Carter wanted to kill Phillips.

But Carter was a professional. He needed Phillips.

Carter took a deep breath and pinned the struggling Phillips down, sat on the heaving chest, pushed the thin muscular arms beneath Carter's incredibly strong legs.

"Need any help?" Elena Markova said sweetly from behind.

"You're late."

Carter sat up, his hands free, and stared down at the twisting, swearing Phillips.

She walked around to where she could see Phillips.

"A pretty sight."

Phillips opened his mouth to complain.

Carter smashed a fist into Phillips's jaw.

For a moment, Phillips looked frustrated. Then he went limp, closed his eyes.

"Damn fine work, N3 . . ."

NICK CARTER IS IT!

"Nick Carter out-Bonds James Bond."
—*Buffalo Evening News*

"Nick Carter is America's #1 espionage agent."
—*Variety*

"Nick Carter is razor-sharp suspense."
—*King Features*

"Nick Carter is extraordinarily big."
—*Bestsellers*

"Nick Carter has attracted an army of addicted readers . . . the books are fast, have plenty of action and just the right degree of sex . . . Nick Carter is the American James Bond, suave, sophisticated, a killer with both the ladies and the enemy."
—*The New York Times*

FROM THE NICK CARTER
KILLMASTER SERIES

NICK CARTER

KILLMASTER

Day of the Mahdi

CHARTER BOOKS, NEW YORK

DAY OF THE MAHDI

A Charter Book/published by arrangement with
The Condé Nast Publications, Inc.

PRINTING HISTORY
Charter Original/July 1984

ISBN: 0-441-13918-3

Charter Books are published by The Berkley Publishing Group,
200 Madison Avenue, New York, New York 10016.
PRINTED IN THE UNITED STATES OF AMERICA

*Dedicated to the men of the
Secret Services of the
United States of America.*

PROLOGUE

Some five hundred miles below Khartoum, the White Nile winds flat and peaceful through forests of acacia, ebony, and mahogany.

There, on a day in the dry season in the southern Sudan, crocodiles lay in a clump, tails in the water, eyes closed against the hot sun. Hippopotami stood submerged on a sandbar in the untroubled river, only their ears and nostrils showing. A gazelle stepped out from the reeds, papyrus, and fragrant frangipani that rimmed the forest and overhung the river. The gazelle glanced at the sleeping crocs, then delicately pushed her nose into the water to drink. Monkeys groomed each other and chattered. Wild parrots screeched. Large blood-sucking seroot flies buzzed. The hippos noisily shot streams of brown river water into the pristine air.

Suddenly the gazelle's head jerked up. The monkeys and parrots stilled. The hippos lifted their massive heads. The crocs opened their eyes and leaned together to stare at the forest.

As if at a signal, the animals and birds vanished into the forest and river.

All was deserted and silent.

Until a man staggered out of the thick forest.

His arms hung loosely at his sides. Branches, reeds, and tangled jungle vegetation ripped at the remains of his three-piece Western suit. He staggered on, eyes half-closed, too weak to lift his hands. He collapsed on a narrow strip of sand at the curve of the bend where he was hidden by flowers and forest on three sides, vulnerable only to the river.

A monkey began to chatter again. Then two, then three. The gazelle returned to finish her drink. The hippos shook their shoulders and waded to their sandbar. The parrots screeched and chased mosquitoes.

The man did not move.

The crocs swam toward the motionless man. The seroot flies landed on his torn flesh. The crocs glided up onto the sand. The flies burrowed into the man's bloody wounds and feasted.

The roar of an approaching motor launch filled the air above the placid water.

The crocs dove for the river. The hippos, monkeys, birds, and gazelle again disappeared. But the seroot flies stayed on, eating their way into the living man, too glutted to notice any threat.

In the launch, a tall, bone-thin Caucasian stood scanning the shore, his constantly moving eyes shaded by a battered, wide-brimmed hat. He searched the riverbank and the forest like a hungry vulture in need of a kill. Low on each hip he wore a Colt Python revolver. His tropical clothes were old and shabby, but the long revolvers gleamed. He had strapped them to his legs, a professional.

Beneath him, squatting in the launch, were two Azandes in dirty white turbans and singlets. Their black skins shone with sweat. They slumped with heat and boredom. One shaved an acacia stick with a long, razor-edged knife. The shavings fell between his naked feet. The other Azande ignored him. The shaver did not know how to carve.

Suddenly the white leader shouted.

The Azandes looked up and then out across the river to where the leader turned the launch. When the Azandes saw the body, they grinned wolfishly. The leader nodded, barked an order, and swung the launch up onto the sand. The three men jumped out, and stopped. They stared at the body on the sand.

"My God! Even wing-tip shoes!" the bone-thin white man said.

"What man do here in those clothes, boss?" the Azande with the knife asked. He kicked the bottom of the body's foot.

The leader looked a moment longer, then shrugged.

"Who knows?" The leader pulled off a gold wedding band from the body's hand. "Gaafar! Dammit, get to work!" He grabbed the other hand and yanked off a platinum watch. Disturbed seroot flies swarmed up around his head, and he waved them off.

Gaafar ran to the body's head and stuck the muzzle of his rifle into its ear.

The other Azande took off the wing-tip shoes and shoved his broad dusty toes into them.

The white leader searched the body in the three-piece Western suit. The pants and jacket had been shredded in the bush, but the pockets were still intact. He avoided the wounds, which were black and thick with flies jockeying like pigs at a trough. He put the wallet, credit cards, papers, money from assorted countries, and a diamond-studded money clip into a pile beside him.

The Azande with the shoes gave up trying to get them on. He glared irritably at the body. Then he grinned and took out his long knife. He licked his thumb, ran it along the blade, and sliced neatly into a thigh wound, flicking flesh and raging flies into the air.

The body screamed. The tall, thin white man laughed. He watched the body's contorted Levantine face with the tightly closed eyes twitch and moan.

The Azande, grinning broadly, raised his knife again. The other Azande spoke softly, encouraging.

"Hey, hey," he said.

But the leader grabbed the raised arm and held it.

The leader bent close to stare at the body's bruised face. He saw thick black eyebrows and a drooping mustache, lightly bearded, smooth cheeks accustomed to a barber-shop and expensive after shave lotion, distinctive white temples probably dyed. But it was the eyes that told him what he had only guessed. The eyes that suddenly shot open in terror, liquid and large and black. Egyptian eyes, famous to a few, that closed almost immediately to sink back into unconsciousness.

The leader snapped up the wallet and pawed through it, grunting his excitement.

"Gaafar, Wari!" he ordered. "The launch!" He jerked his thumb at the body on the sand. The Azandes, disappointed, picked up the Egyptian and threw him into the launch.

The doctor was old, tired, and reeked of daily whiskey, but he knew what to do. He had the Egyptian's feet elevated above the head. A nurse with curled lips cleaned the wounds of flies, eggs, and excrement. Two intravenous tubes ran together into the right arm. The doctor was using the best of the equipment in the bush hospital and the only hospital bed for three hundred miles around. But then, he was the only doctor for five hundred miles and could do what he liked.

The doctor wiped sweat shakily from his forehead and upper lip.

"Phillips," he said, "bring me that basin."

The tall white man, Phillips, carried the chipped porcelain basin half full of thin green liquid to a table beside the Egyptian. The doctor washed his hands in the basin and shook them in the air.

"Ran out of sterile gloves two weeks ago," he said. "Can't trust the laundry to get anything clean. One fat woman with a rock. That's the laundry. Not like Montreal, eh? And I wanted to grow up to be Albert Schweitzer." He laughed alone at his joke.

The doctor's hands moved slowly over the Egyptian, feeling, poking, prodding. The Egyptian moaned, and the doctor shook his head.

"Damned glad I've got antibiotics." He glanced at Phillips. "All that fly shit in him . . . must've found him on the river."

Phillips nodded. "When can he talk?"

"Shock, infection, dehydration. Maybe brain damage. Don't know if he'll ever talk again."

"Make him."

The doctor straightened up and stared at Phillips. He spoke to the nurse in dialect without looking at her.

"You're done, girl. Roll him on his side and get back to the ward."

The nurse scuttled around Phillips, avoiding the Python revolvers, and ran out the door. Phillips drew one of the big pistols, savoring the balance. He pointed it at the doctor.

"Now."

"Kill me, and he'll *never* talk." The doctor returned to his patient, and the skilled hands worked shakily over the Egyptian's back. "You are a bastard, aren't you, Phillips?" The whiskey voice was contemptuous. "Never a thought for people. Guns, ivory, white and black slavery—that's it. You'd sell your best friend, if you had any to . . . ahhh, what's this?"

Phillips snatched the aluminum container from the doctor's hand.

"I wouldn't be too quick if I were you," the doctor said. "Came from the anus. We know about that, don't we? Old prison smuggling trick. Could be anything. Diamonds to cocaine to poison gas. Amazing what—"

"Shut up!"

Phillips twisted open the container and pulled out a scrap of paper. The doctor watched as he opened it and then leaned over to read it himself.

"See that seal?" the doctor asked. "Egyptian government stamp. Even more reason you should let the poor . . ."

Phillips raised the Colt Python again, anticipation puffing his thin face like an adder's.

"Too bad you had to recognize that seal."

"I told you," the doctor said, stepping back, now alarmed, "your Egyptian won't live if I'm not—"

Phillips shot the doctor in the mouth, a surprised mouth that shattered with brains and cartilage into a thick, sticky mist that hazed the whitewashed room in pink. Large pieces of bone and flesh stuck to the Egyptian, the porcelain basin, and the walls and floor. The bullet exited through the doctor's occipital bone, blowing the top of his head off.

Phillips looked at the paper again. Besides the government seal, there were five words: *Day of the Mahdi . . . Nyala: . . .* Whatever else had been on the paper had been torn away before the paper was put into the canister.

Phillips glanced down at the doctor, saw blood still pumping from the remaining skull. He smiled slightly and swung out of the hospital compound. The Nilotic natives hid behind door cloths and baobab trees until he passed. Then they swarmed back into the long wooden hospital hut, wailing.

The one-room shack had subtle moist odors that came from the packed dirt floor and the stripped mahogany pole walls. The room was dark, shaded by thick castor oil plants that Phillips had grown close around the shack to hide it from lost natives and even more from lost whites. The castor oil plants were healthy, twenty feet high, the leaves two to three feet wide and ornamental enough to be the envy of even the most discerning florist. Phillips liked that.

He paused only a moment to let his eyes adjust. Then he walked three long steps forward, sat his skeletal frame onto a campstool, and bent over an old but powerful radio.

ONE

It was ten o'clock at night, and Nick Carter put out his sixtieth cigarette of the day. He smiled smoothly and nodded his way through customs at the Riyadh airport. Expertly forged credentials and a cover story that checks to the remotest aunt and bookkeeper are helpful, but never enough. A certain amount of arrogance did the real job.

Carrying his briefcase, he blended with the chaotic crowd of tourists and pilgrims following signs through the concourse toward the relief of individual taxicabs.

Arabic music and recitations from the Koran mingled in the airport's public areas, coming from cassette recorders carried in the arms of fully veiled Muslim women and white- and brown-robed Muslim men. Most of the children, clinging to the hands of their traditionally dressed parents, wore sundresses or sunsuits with designer labels from Paris. Occasionally there were Bedouin National Guardsmen with the distinctive hot odor and gleam of the desert. They wore red-and-white kaffiyehs with the official emblem of the kingdom—crossed swords and a palm—pinned on their black headbands.

There is a point for even the most professional traveler, usually just after debarkation, where the crush of bodies, the cloying of stale air conditioning, and the visual changes of geography and customs become overwhelming. Then the excitement of the job at hand is lost in the headlong rush for a drink—if one is not Muslim or Mormon—solitude, and rest.

Nick Carter reflected on this as he suddenly felt his exhaustion. He increased his attentiveness, and watched the alien eyes and hands and silent airport shadows for a portent of danger. He added more spring to his stride and focused his extraordinary intellect on his assignment. He was Killmaster N3 of AXE, the ultrasecret U.S. agency, the smallest and most deadly arm of American global intelligence—and he had never failed. Yet.

It was the "yet" that put the smile to his lean, handsome face as he slipped around an ordinary corner, out an unmarked door, and into the night desert heat of the royal capital of Saudi Arabia.

He breathed deeply of the hot dry air and listened as jet engines warmed up and taxied off. The "yet" was the challenge—old-fashioned, but it was still what kept humanity forging forward to better itself. It was the anticipation of inevitable competition, even against one's self. He thought this as he moved through shadows, around an airport bulldozer, into the dark of a deserted hangar, past jets, airplanes, platforms, and parts, and into a dim, air-conditioned business office. When he closed the door, the walls rattled. Flimsy construction was worldwide. At least the whine of the jets was not as loud inside.

"You have it, N3?" The voice was appropriately low-keyed and controlled, even deferential as befitted Carter's reputation and rank. It came from a figure in a black veil and robe standing in a corner beside the only furniture in the room, a metal desk and chair.

Carter nodded. There was a quiet click. His stiletto, Hugo, jumped silently, unobtrusively, into his hand. He stepped forward on the balls of his feet. He grinned.

"You do look good in that dress," Carter murmured, Hugo hidden in his hand.

"No games, N3." The voice had changed, was deeper. "Hand it over."

"Of course."

Carter jammed Hugo up under the robed figure's rib cage, grabbing the hand beneath the robe while the other clawed uselessly at Hugo. He twisted the pencil-thin stiletto, and hot blood bathed his hand.

"No games," Carter said to the shocked eyes that now stared back uncomprehendingly. "No rules."

The blood was thickening on his hand. He held the stiletto in place a moment longer to be sure, and then, releasing Hugo, caught the body as it slumped. Gently, he lowered it to the floor where it rested in its own blood.

Carter pulled a kit from his oiled leather briefcase. First he cleaned Hugo. Killmasters have great respect for their equipment. It is one of the reasons they live long enough to grow good enough to be Killmasters. Besides Hugo, Carter relied on Wilhelmina, a 9mm Luger, and Pierre, a tiny gas bomb.

Once clean, he slipped Hugo back into its chamois sheath on his arm from where, with the flick of the wrist, it would again slide instantly and noiselessly into his palm.

He wiped his hands and face, then inspected his navy suit in the darkness. His sensitive fingers found the rough spots where blood had dried. He took off the jacket, removed a tiny nylon envelope from the briefcase, and shook out the black jumpsuit made of an experimental—it was air-light with the tensile strength of steel—fabric. He could not be seen wearing bloodstained clothes. He stepped into the new coveralls.

And in a single, smooth, unhurried movement, Nick Carter stopped, crouched, slid the tiny gas bomb from his inner thigh, and crab walked the four steps to the three-by-three closed office window. He held the bomb loose and comfortable in his hand, and flattened himself against the flimsy wall.

The faint sound had come from outside the single window of the dim little office.

TWO

A shadow—slight, fast, and expert—darted across the tarmac. It must have been beneath the office window since before Carter arrived. Now there was nothing. Carter pulled out Wilhelmina, searching the softly shadowed desert night.

Did the intruder know? What did he know? And how . . . ?

From his pocket, Carter took a suction cup with an attached plastic handle and what looked like a roll of striated nylon tape. He watched the tarmac while he noiselessly attached the suction cup to the center of the window. He pressed the tape along the inside perimeter of the windowpane until the glass was completely outlined. Then he scraped his thumbnail over the striations. Instantly there was intense heat, crackling, and the stink of ozone. He picked up the glass by the suction cup's handle and laid it noiselessly on the floor. It was lumped and beaded along the edges. The room filled with airport noises.

Carter raised Wilhelmina.

The shadow was back, small and cautious.

It was returning to the window.

Carter needed only a moment to get a sighting.

"The AXE tattoo is on your inner elbow, N3." The clear whisper carried across the tarmac. "Hawk wouldn't like you to shoot me."

Carter froze. No one should know who he was, or the names "AXE" and "Hawk," unless—

10

"Where does the eagle fly?"

"Higher than the sparrow, lower than the hawk," the voice answered, still not moving. It had a British accent.

"Who are you?"

The shadow walked away from the black pit that was a wall, around another bulldozer, and into the dim airport light. Carter backed away from the window to watch a short, dapper man in his early seventies step agilely through the window and into the office.

A Killmaster is seldom surprised. Surprise can often be fatal. But life can be boring without surprises, and the premier Killmaster, Nick Carter, enjoyed occasional indulgences.

Amused, he watched the elderly gentleman glance at the robed body on the floor and then stand ramrod straight, as if reporting in. The seventy-year-old had a round, florid face with a bushy, cavalryman's mustache below an arched nose and sharp, clear blue eyes. He wore riding breeches, boots, and an Arab burnoose that hung loose and open. On his white head was a kaffiyeh, worn jauntily, as if he had earned it. He considered the body for a time.

"How did you figure it out, old boy?" he asked in his clipped Oxbridge accent.

"Wahhabis aren't blond. And then I heard the click."

The British gentleman noted the yellow hairs on the back of the one hand that showed.

"Quite."

"MI6?" Carter asked.

"Five, actually. Retired. But I keep my hand in, you know. Every eye and ear helps. I don't have much time. My chaps got word you were due here, put me onto you on the instructions of your superior . . . someone named Hawk, eh?" Idly, the toe of his boot flicked open the robe of the body on the floor.

"The click," he said thoughtfully. "Nasty little trick, that."

Carter smiled. "I thought so."

They looked at the cocked cyanide pistol in the hand

that was cooling toward rigor mortis.

Carter asked, "You don't have time for what,
Mr. . . . ?"

"Young. Cecil Young." He stroked his luxuriant mustache. "I'm not all that damned sure what it is, but it's
something that puts the wind up. I smell it, eh?" Cecil
Young looked at the metal desk and chair. He frowned. "I
do abhor a Spartan office." He pulled out the chair,
leaned back in it, and propped his feet up on the desk. He
pulled the folds of his burnoose in front of him and clasped
his hands. He looked himself over, pleased with the im-
provement. "It's a good story, chappie. Just two events.
Do sit down. I'll make it quick."

Carter's eyes checked the room. If Cecil Young had
come through Hawk, the information must be important.
Would it change Hawk's orders? Perhaps even the kill?
He sat on the desk, his back to the wall.

"Tell me what you smell, Mr. Young."

"Cecil. And I shall call you Nicky. In this business, we
don't have time for the customary formalities. Efficiency
and moderation, that's what makes a civilized man. And a
civilized country."

Carter grinned. Cecil Young, despite his protestations,
was not to be hurried. Did Hawk know what he'd sent?

"Cecil, then."

"Right-o." Young stroked his bushy silver mustache
again and thought. "It all began with Teddy. Teddy's the
prime minister here, one of King Abdul Aziz al-Saud's
boys. Old Ibn Saud to you, I expect. All the kings and
PMs since Abdul Aziz died in 1953 have been his sons.
Don't recall offhand how many boys he had." Young
looked expectantly at Carter.

The old fox was testing him.

"Thirty-four surviving sons and dozens of daughters.
There's never been an official count of the daughters."

Young nodded, clear blue eyes twinkling. Carter knew
there would be at least one more pause in the conversation, and he looked forward to the challenge. An agent
should know the country he was in, but only the best did.

Carter took out his cigarette case and opened it.

"As you may be aware," Young continued, watching Carter light one of his custom-made cigarettes, "Abdul Aziz sent his boys to be educated in the West. Teddy came down from Oxford. Unfortunately for him, he discovered while there that although his spirit seemed puritan Wahhabi, his body enjoyed dissoluteness. Teddy liked to binge-drink, old boy. Not often, but occasionally and secretly. When he returned to Saudi Arabia, I struck up a friendship with him. My cover was horse breeder. He owned a chain of stables stocked with purebred Arabians, and he needed someone reliable to drink with here. We've been drinking together sub rosa for years. London had picked him out as a boy with a future. Astoundingly, the pencil pushers were right. It looks as if he'll be the next king. As for his politics . . . Nicky, you wouldn't happen to know anything about Teddy's politics, would you?"

"Some." Carter flicked his cigarette ash. "He and King Fahd are both strong moderates, pro-Western, and committed to justice for Palestine, not just to 'Middle East peace.' Because of their religion, they're very anti-Communist. They've traditionally based their security on U.S.-British military support. Their Arab neighbors are more radical and more ready to fight. The Saudis want a comprehensive Middle East settlement—and that means for Palestine, too. The problem is Israel as well as the other Arab countries. Jews and Arabs—two hounds quarreling over the same bone—but the Saudis are more willing to compromise. And your PM, Teddy, follows those politics right down the line."

"I say, Nicky"—Cecil Young's face was a mask, passive, but the eyes twinkled even more now as they silently approved Carter's knowledge—"you wouldn't mind if I had one of your burners, would you? They do smell awfully good. No one knows how to make decent burners these days."

Carter opened the cigarette case again and the septuagenarian reached a steady hand in. Very rarely did an agent so highly and dangerously placed as Cecil Young live to such an impressive age. Carter lit the old agent's cigarette.

"Thanks, Nicky," Young said. "Now to the scent. As I said, it all began with Teddy. He got quite intoxicated three nights ago. I try to hold it down for myself, although I'm not always successful. Depends on how watchful he is. He does like his camaraderie. Anyway, Teddy's big topic was the wonderful development that his—and the king's, of course—younger half brother, Mujahid, has finally come to his senses. Mujahid is a religious fanatic, a demented zealot, who loves to chop off criminals' hands and heads. Teddy says that Mujahid is going to come in off the desert to join the king and the other brothers at a great meeting. It's more than they'd ever hoped for from Mujahid. This meeting—now hold on to your seat, it's a bit of a shocker—is to seriously consider official recognition of Israel. Imagine that. And with maybe the zealot Mujahid's blessing."

Cecil Young sat back to smoke, his white head in the kaffiyeh cocked, thoughtful. "Nicky, I don't believe in these sudden changes of heart. I think Teddy and the king are being led down the proverbial garden path. They do want a peaceful settlement—but more, the triumph of worldwide recognition of the superiority of their policies. What I don't know yet is why Mujahid is pretending to change his mind—it's not kindness or right thinking—and to what purpose."

Carter nodded, reassessing his assignment.

Cecil Young studied the cigarette he held. He smoked, blew three rings into the air in quick succession. "You have class, Nicky. Of course I noticed it instantly, the gold initials embossed on these filters. It's dangerous, lad. But then you know that. Must be quite a brain-bender to talk yourself out of the 'N.C.' when your cover names have different initials."

Carter laughed. "Yes, sir. But life is to be lived, not hidden from." He put out his cigarette and dropped the butt inside a sliding panel at the bottom of the gold cigarette case. "And the second event?"

"Exactly. Something else I can't explain. Makes the hairs on the back of the neck stand up. It's about an Iraqi firebrand colonel named Ahmad al-Barzani. Know him?"

"I've seen his picture. A national hero. Made a reputation for himself when he stood up against the Kurdish rebels a few years back. He didn't have much support."

Cecil Young nodded. "He also was one of the few who fought skillfully and bravely in the early days of the war against Iran. But he's not been given a command in a long time. One wonders why. And the Saudis weren't terribly friendly to the whole Iraq-Iran War, to either side, and certainly not to specific Iraqi military men, nevertheless I saw al-Barzani in Riyadh yesterday. I know it was him. And he was dressed like a Bedouin camel driver, right down to the stench. You know they throw their clothes at the camels when the beasts get enraged? Saw it once. Damned camel stomped, chewed, spat, and pissed on the driver's clothes. When the fit was over, the poor bloke put the stinking rags right back on and man and beast were merrily off, all grudges forgiven. Extraordinary. Anyway, I looked al-Barzani right in the eyes yesterday, and he didn't blink. Interesting man, that. Don't think he had the faintest, but then his line is slightly different, isn't it?"

Cecil Young ground out his cigarette on the sole of his boot and handed the butt to Carter to dispose of.

"Did you . . ." Carter started, and stopped as a large jet, probably a DC-10, roared into life.

The Killmaster and the retired MI5 agent smiled and shrugged. They would wait.

Then the wall across from them caved in.

And was caught like confetti in the scoop of a bulldozer that rolled straight at them.

"Cadmus founded Thebes, goddamnit!" Phillips shouted into the radio. "What's wrong with you idiots?"

He pounded the table as he waited again for someone to answer who would know his priority.

"Cadmus introduced the alphabet into Greece," came the response at last.

"Where the hell have you been, Hawk?" Phillips growled. "You quitting or just turning senile?"

"It's good to talk to you, too, Phillips." Hawk's voice was heavy with sarcasm. "What have you got for me?"

"Maybe nothing. Depends on what you're paying."

"Standard rates. If that bores you, sell it elsewhere. Then we'll steal it. Slower but less distasteful."

Phillips drummed his fingers and smiled a thin-lipped smile that bared his teeth. "It's from Egypt. It's good."

"Convince me."

"How does Major General Gamal Farouk, head of the Egyptian secret police, strike you?"

"Just a minute, Phillips."

He'd got Hawk's attention and now the radio was silent. Phillips leaned back in his campstool, crossed his arms, and thought. Hawk was an arrogant son of a bitch. You'd think Yanks would encourage free enterprise instead of being so bloody righteous about who they did business with. Trudeau had been right. Having the United States for a neighbor was like sleeping with an elephant. Every time it grunted, you paid attention and prayed it wouldn't roll over. For a moment, Phillips smelled the hot baguettes and croissants of his native Montreal. He saw the fresh butter, heard the cooing accents, and ran down the red brick street, away from . . .

"Farouk is missing." Hawk was back. "Air crash. He and the pilot."

"The pilot I don't know about. Farouk I found on the White Nile."

"Alive?"

"Enough. With a message in a canister stuck up his ass."

"Who knows about it?"

Phillips barked a laugh.

"Are you kidding? You know me better than that. No one knows," Phillips said complacently. "Now, how much is it worth to you?"

He could almost hear Hawk sigh.

"I don't know the message, therefore I can't judge its value."

"It has the Egyptian government stamp on it: *Most Secret*."

There was only hesitation.

"How much do you want?" Hawk asked.

"Ten thousand. Credited to my Swiss account within twenty-four hours. If it's not, I kill Farouk. Then I pin it on you."

"You are a gentle man, Phillips. No doubt the apple of your mother's eye."

Phillips laughed bitterly.

"Do you want the message or not?" Phillips snapped.

"Read it to me."

THREE

Two men sprang from each side of the bulldozer. The four were Bedouins, robed in white, swinging long swords that gleamed menacingly in the gloom.

There is an instant of shock after the completely unexpected happens. It can stretch to thirty seconds or more for the average person. Long enough for a fatal automobile accident. Long enough for a crippling fall down a cliff. Long enough for a bulldozer going at full speed to crush all in its path.

The Bedouins' berserk cries swelled in the air.

The bulldozer's blade advanced.

Nick Carter moved first.

With his lightning-quick overhand, Cárter sent Hugo slicing through the darkness and into the carotid artery of the bulldozer's driver. The driver shot up out of his seat, desperately trying to hold his throat together. Blood gushed out in a geyser that soaked the white-robed driver and covered the steering wheel. The bulldozer stalled and stopped.

The Bedouins screamed and swung their long swords above their heads.

"Religious fanatics, old boy!" Cecil Young shouted and pulled a service revolver from his burnoose.

A Bedouin brought his long sword down, and Cecil Young moved just in time so that he lost only his revolver.

Carter kicked the Bedouin in the belly. He felt the satisfactory crush of stomach and intestines. The Bedouin squealed and doubled over. Carter smoothly swiveled

18

away. Cecil Young pulled a metal drawer from the desk and slammed the Bedouin's face to the floor. Blood spread into a lake around the head.

Carter moved in on the other three, dodging the swinging swords, and jammed his fist into the groin of one Bedouin followed by a brutal uppercut that knocked the Bedouin deep into the confetti of the bulldozer's blade.

Cecil Young picked up the first Bedouin's sword and, swinging it above his head as if he were born to it, bellowed in Arabic:

"There is no god but God! Muhammad is the messenger of God!"

The last two Bedouins spun to attack Young.

Carter yanked down the black headband of one and snapped it across the neck in a powerful contraction that broke the man's voicebox. The Bedouin tore at the headband, his mouth open in a soundless scream. Carter threw him out the window.

The bulldozer roared to life and jerked toward them. The Bedouin who had been thrown into the blade's confetti had crawled up and now sat in the dead driver's seat, his face bruised and ugly with hate as he bore the big machine down on them.

Young suddenly stepped aside as the last standing Bedouin thrust and whirled. Young parried and, grinning, pushed his sword through the Bedouin's belly and out the back. He stepped close to the skewered Bedouin, breathing up into the dark desert face, and grinned again.

"My sword of righteousness," he explained in Arabic and kicked the Bedouin off.

Airport security sirens squealed over the sounds of the bulldozer and the idling jets. The bulldozer advanced closer.

They looked at the bodies.

"These are that rotter Mujahid's boys," Cecil Young said. "Poor Teddy's going to have his hands full this time. I knew something was up. Haven't lost my touch, old chap."

Cecil Young adjusted his kaffiyeh. Nick Carter dusted

his black jumpsuit, picked up his briefcase, and pulled out Wilhelmina. The bulldozer was almost upon them.

"Can I give you a lift, Nicky?" Mr. Cecil Young asked.

"Thank you, sir. I would enjoy that."

Nick Carter lifted the 9mm Luger and shot the determined Bedouin bulldozer driver between the eyes. It was a clean hole, a third eye, lashless and black. An enormous bubble of blood appeared and spread down across the disappointed face. Nick Carter raised Wilhelmina in salute, and he and Young exited through the window.

FOUR

Flat brown desert, oil wells, and the edge of the blue Persian Gulf spread below the jet's window. The sand gave up a glazed sheen in the heat. Black specks, probably Bedouins, snaked across the Nejd toward a water hole where they would pitch colorful tents, eat hard bread, and drink the traditional, bitter, cardomom-flavored coffee.

Nick Carter turned from the window and put earphones over his head. He was flying from Riyadh to Baghdad, tailing Colonel Ahmad al-Barzani. The unsuspecting colonel sat six seats ahead, now dressed as an Anglican bishop. The disguise was strangely believable despite the Iraqi face. Al-Barzani wore the foreign clerical collar and robes with unselfconscious dignity, as he must have worn the camel driver's rags Cecil Young had described. Either disguise would be secondary to al-Barzani. It was the man who was primary. Al-Barzani was so self-confident that, no matter what he wore, he was the same and therefore authentic whether in rags or robes.

Nick Carter considered this as he got out the small machine that looked like a tape recorder. Authenticity was an essential but often overlooked ingredient to greatness—or to ineffectual eccentricity. Carter wondered which it was with al-Barzani as he balanced the "recorder" on his muscled thigh, punched "Play," and adjusted the earphones. The machine was powered by a minigenerator and plugged into AXE's worldwide computer through a special radio-telephone hookup. After a few clicks, he heard the computer's sultry voice.

"Yes, N3? What is your pleasure?"

"Not you, baby," Carter murmured absently to the sexy electronic voice that was one of Hawk's jokes. He punched a question on the machine's hidden keyboard. "Sorry to disappoint you."

As he waited for the computer to respond, he smiled at the veiled Muslim woman across the aisle. She lowered her head demurely to examine the soft ringed hands folded in her lap. She might be curious about the handsome Western man who muttered to himself, but her religious training forbade her the boldness to move from shy glances to bashful questions.

"Colonel Ahmad Fazlollah al-Barzani," the computer suddenly purred with enthusiasm. "The colonel was born in a small village outside Qaiyara on the Tigris River in northern Iraq. His father was a herder. As a boy, Ahmad was recognized as unusually bright, and the tribal elder ordered that he be sent into Qaiyara to school. Very little else is known of his early years. By the time he reached the University of Baghdad, he had a reputation for a brilliant mind, hot temper, and puritanical religious fervor. He is a devout Muslim of the Shiah sect. Once, as a university student, he reportedly nearly beat to death a more liberal male friend who was considering marrying a Muslim woman of the Sunni sect. The friend repented, and after recovery, made atonement by marrying three women—all Shiites.

"After graduation, al-Barzani joined the army. He was wounded twice in the 1967 Arab-Israeli War and insisted on returning each time to fight again on the Jordan-Israeli border. In 1968 he supported Major General Ahmed Hassan al-Bakr's overthrow of the Iraqi government and the subsequent hostility to the West and friendship to the Soviet Union. Al-Barzani rose slowly through the ranks until 1974 when he fought against the Kurds in northern Iraq, eventually commanding the famous Zab Brigade. The Kurds, mostly Sunni Muslims who live on both sides of the border between Iraq and Iran, were fighting for more autonomy. During this minor war, al-Barzani was promoted from major to lieutenant colonel to full colonel in less than four months because he discovered secret Iranian materiel aid flowing to the Kurds. Al-Barzani then systematically cut all Iran-Kurd supply lines and kept them inoperative. This forced an end to the Kurds' revolt.

"In the early days of the Iran-Iraq border dispute of 1980-81, he fought bravely and was decorated again. A series of three photographs taken of him by an Associated Press photographer appeared in newspapers around the world. The series shows him leading a charge near the river Shatt-al-Arab in which his men are deserting until, in the third photo, he is running alone, a grenade held high in his hand. Fighting in battle is, of course, very unusual for an officer of his rank, but al-Barzani has his own way of doing things. He went on to single-handedly explode an antiaircraft gun emplacement and kill the six Iranians who were defending it with machine guns. Afterward, he asked to be relieved and was returned to a desk job in Baghdad. It was rumored that his change of heart was due to a religious vision in which he saw that he was killing his spiritual brothers—in other words, other Shiite Muslims.

"Al-Barzani has remained in the army but has fallen into disfavor. This is because despite his record of bravery, he is now an embarrassment to the Iraqi government. His growing impatience that the Shiites assume their rightful places over the Sunnites as the dominant Muslim sect in the Arab world has made him more and more outspoken, and he has apparently refused several assignments that the military thought him particularly necessary for. Al-Barzani is expected to ask for early retirement from the army to assume official leadership of other religiously conservative Iraqis who now support Iran. Iran's Ayatollah Khoumeni is the epitome of the Shiites' idea of leadership—forceful and righteous. Al-Barzani has the same religious purity and leadership qualities as the Ayatollah, and is certainly the Ayatollah's military and intellectual superior. Altogether, al-Barzani is potentially a very dangerous man."

The computer voice paused, then the machine asked

solicitously, "Is there anything else I can do for you, N3?"

Nick Carter laughed and pushed the "Stop/Eject" button.

"Computers are nothing without people," Carter said in English, smiling at the shy, veiled woman across the aisle. He packed the earphones and "recorder" into his briefcase.

"I beg your pardon?" the woman said in Arabic.

"It's of no importance," he responded in Arabic. "A mere bagatelle." Carter had worked hard on his Arabic before going on this assignment and was pleased with his new fluency. He leaned back and lit a cigarette.

"What is this . . . bagatelle?" Her head lifted and he felt the veiled eyes upon him.

Muslim men, bearded, turned to stare at Carter and the woman.

"Bagatelle means trifle." He smoked and watched the flowing movements of the woman with the soft hands and young voice. "It's French, originally the name of a board game. Do you know about board games?"

"Oh, yes," she replied quickly. "My husband and I play often with his mother. 'Monopoly.' 'Clue.' I do like to play games . . . don't you?"

A Muslim man, sitting directly behind Carter, hissed. Others moved angrily in their seats and glared at Carter and the Muslim woman. Carter was glad there were no stones to be had on the jet.

"Especially," he told the woman as he watched al-Barzani rise from his seat ahead, "when a prize well worth the winning hangs in the balance."

"Oh!" The woman's sigh was sharp, a breathy gasp.

Al-Barzani's Anglican robes blocked the aisle, and he leaned over to whisper to the woman. She shrank into the corner. Al-Barzani turned, his dark face, sharply hooked nose, and black burning eyes on Carter.

"Perhaps you do not know the religious customs of this woman's people," al-Barzani said pleasantly in English as his eyes burned warning. "It is forbidden for women to fraternize with men outside their families. That is why buses and trains are partitioned. Unfortunately''—he looked casually up and down the jet's narrow aisle, pausing to engage and dismiss the few Western eyes he met— "airplanes cannot accommodate the separation of sexes, so we of other beliefs must remember a partition exists.'' The hot eyes looked directly at Carter. "Do you understand?''

Nick Carter smoked and smiled.

"Absolutely,'' he said.

Al-Barzani was smooth and controlled in the disguise that had little meaning to him. Only the burning eyes showed zealotry, and zealots had short fuses. Carter wondered which was stronger, the smooth control or the burning zealotry.

"These Muslims are barbaric. Don't you agree, Bishop?'' Carter tapped his cigarette in the ashtray and looked up.

An angry flush rose above the clerical collar. "The Koran says: 'Ye are the best of peoples, evolved for mankind. Enjoining what is right, forbidding what is wrong, and believing in God.' Christians would do well to strive for such perfection.''

"I'm sure *you* do, Bishop. I'm sure *you* set a good *Christian* example.'' Carter watched al-Barzani's fists clench and unclench. "Unlike these savages here.''

Al-Barzani's struggle was magnificent. His face with the hooked nose turned beet red. His thick-lipped mouth trembled while the clenched fists pinned the clerical robes to his sides. Then he bared his teeth and slid a hand beneath the robes.

Hugo flipped silently into Nick Carter's hand.

Three beeps sounded over the jet's intercom and Fasten Your Seat Belts and No Smoking signs appeared above the seats.

Al-Barzani looked up, then seemed to mentally shake himself. The hand came out of the robes empty and scratched his ear.

"We're about to land,'' the bishop said, his voice paternal. "*Pax vobiscum*, my son.''

•　•　•

Twenty feet ahead of al-Barzani, Nick Carter carried his briefcase down the causeway that led to Iraqi customs. Al-Barzani was as interesting in person as the AXE computer readout had suggested: the herder's son who graduated from a large university; the military hero who fell from favor; the religious man who was on his way to becoming a religious leader. And now Carter could add one more attribute: the zealot who had self-control. The last made al-Barzani a man of immense personal power and extremely dangerous to those who opposed him. With al-Barzani's natural sense of authenticity, this might easily lead to greatness.

Carter moved forward in line. The Muslim woman from the jet passed through customs ahead of him, a large, turquoise, Samsonite cosmetics case in her hand, and walked into a restroom.

Behind Carter, al-Barzani stood patiently in his clerical robes, waiting his turn in line.

Why had al-Barzani not shown his military credentials? Al-Barzani would have gotten preferential treatment and been whisked through customs. Retaining the disguise made no sense unless the military didn't want the trip known publicly in Iraq . . . or al-Barzani himself didn't want it known.

Carter showed his passport to an expressionless clerk, smiled graciously, and walked unquestioned into the terminal. Ahead of him, a group of Iraqi soldiers were gathering. There were ten of them, their uniforms freshly laundered and pressed, the seams sharp, the pants smooth, and everything from belt buckles to insignia that could be oiled or polished to a glossy sheen had been. On their shoulders were orange patches with a flowing bright blue river, a soaring bird, and the word "Zab."

Carter walked to a newsstand, bought a *Wall Street Journal*, snapped it open to the stock quotations, and, apparently immersed in the businessman's tip sheet, watched the oblivious al-Barzani.

If al-Barzani would soon assume leadership of the pro-Iranian fanatical element in Iraq, what had he been doing in Saudi Arabia, where the Ayatollah and Iran were not at all popular and, for that matter, neither was Iraq? And was he as blind to Westerners as he appeared to be? He'd not tumbled to Cecil Young, and he'd shown no interest in Nick Carter beyond his being a Western man crossing the line with a Muslim woman. Then . . . . al-Barzani's disguises must be for the benefit of other Muslims.

Three officers joined the ten spit-and-polish soldiers. The officers too were dressed impeccably and wore the shoulder patches of the Zab Brigade, the brigade al-Barzani had commanded during his startling series of promotions in the war against the Kurds. One of the three officers was impatiently watching the restroom door and checking his watch.

What had al-Barzani been doing in Saudi Arabia, where the Wahhabis of the hated Sunni sect ruled? Perhaps it was to meet with Shiites unhappy with an impure government, a government that discriminated against them.

A striking blonde with a model's high cheekbones and a cover girl's legs walked out of the ladies' restroom.

Carter realized he'd not noticed the blonde go in, despite the long time he'd spent in line observing, and he would have noticed anyone with her magnetic good looks. Yet there was something familiar about her. . . .

She dropped her small cosmetics case as the young Zab Brigade officer who had been watching the restroom ran to her. She threw her arms around him. He picked her up and whirled her around, his head back, laughing the way a man laughs when he has his woman and he is sure. The blonde laughed too, although it was suddenly clear to Carter that it was only enough to make it look good. Carter watched the woman's graceful, flowing movements. Some people's movements are as distinctive as fingerprints. The cosmetics case was small enough to have fit inside the turquoise case the Muslim woman from the jet had carried into the restroom. Carter had once again found his daring Muslim woman, and her veil and all pretense of shyness were gone. The couple waited off to the side of the two other officers and the group of soldiers.

Al-Barzani was at last through customs, his robes flapping as he strode to the Zab contingent. He shook hands all around, nodded to the blonde—not an unfriendly nod, but not yet accepting—and then, surrounded by his supporters as if they were his guards, he set a fast pace through the airport toward the street. The officer and the blonde trotted to keep up, their arms entwined.

Carter followed the group to the outside curb where Iraqis hawked hand-knotted rugs and multicolored bolts of cloth. He lingered in the airport's shadows as the group piled into three private limousines. Even the blonde got in, unquestioned, as if expected by the swarthy Arab soldiers.

Carter stared at her hard, the profile on the other side of the rolled-down window.

And grinned.

Her movements weren't familiar only from the jet, but from the past. His past. Once she had been an equally striking brunette.

The three limousines drove off, and Carter hailed a taxi. The blonde was Elena Markova, KGB agent. Why was she interested in al-Barzani?

Carter had made the right decision in tailing al-Barzani. Something was going on, and since the KGB was involved, Hawk would want to know what it was.

FIVE

The al-Barzani party drove past the stalls of a giant bazaar crowded with people, goods, and the enthusiasm of a healthy business climate, and then past the ruins of Bab al-Watani, the famous ancient gates of Baghdad now restored as an arms museum. At last the limousines stopped before a nondescript red brick building near the Tigris. Soldiers snapped to attention on either side of the double entrance doors and al-Barzani—now dressed splendidly as an Iraqi colonel—stepped onto the sidewalk.

From across the street, Carter watched al-Barzani speak to the soldiers who gathered at the entrance. Occasionally the colonel put a friendly hand on a shoulder or told a joke. The soldiers laughed, happy, charmed by the leader who was so much one of them yet remained obviously in command.

Elena Markova and her young officer again stood off to the side, respectfully observing, and when Colonel al-Barzani finally entered the building—obviously his headquarters—the young couple slipped away and down the sidewalk toward the Tigris.

There was no other officer of al-Barzani's rank or higher near the narrow brick building. There was no official—or unofficial—sign to declare the building's purpose to the public. Who was paying for al-Barzani's headquarters? And to what purpose?

Elena Markova's officer dropped her hand and put his arm possessively around her waist, urging her down the sidewalk.

Carter watched them. He could manage his way into the headquarters, probably get into the files. He could call Hawk; Carter had been on the move since Riyadh and still hadn't had a chance to check in to find out what Hawk had intended by sending Cecil Young with information but no instructions. Or he could tail Elena Markova.

Carter watched Elena's slim hips disappear down the sidewalk beside the officer's bulk. She was a walking trap. The KGB used her only in worst-case situations, just as AXE used Nick Carter only in worst-case situations.

Carter picked up his briefcase from the shadow of a doorway. Al-Barzani, the headquarters, and Hawk would keep. Elena Markova could be a shortcut to answers.

Like any businessman-tourist, Carter adjusted his tie and sauntered down the sidewalk as if to gaze at the strange sights.

He followed the couple along the Tigris where Iraqis paddled *gufas*. The round boats made of wickerwork had been used in Mesopotamia for countless centuries, carrying food, goods for trading, and tourists charmed by the improbability of their floating. Perhaps even Cleopatra had been charmed.

Carter crossed the street and stood quietly at an intersection. Elena and her officer had entered an expensive, modern highrise of glass and steel with fake balconies appended to the windows like false eyelashes. Carter walked past the building, saw through the glass doors the couple entering an elevator, their heads together, the officer's hand on Elena's lightly covered round ass.

Carter walked past the building again, and this time he paid attention to the broad, tall—at least six and a half feet—doorman who walked the lobby, bored. The doorman was dressed like a Turkoman, with a thick fur hat and belted coat. He was a security guard, the muscles in his fleshy face and the discontented eyes said, and he knew he should be grateful. The job was air conditioned and easy.

Nick Carter pushed through the glass entry doors and into the lobby.

"*As-Salaam alaykum*," Carter said, walking over to the lobby desk and setting down his briefcase.

The doorman watched with interest.

"And upon you, peace," he said in Arabic. "But I cannot let you in if your name is not on my list."

"It's wise you said that," Carter said and opened the briefcase. "I'm from Aramco. We've just bought this property."

"What?"

The guard's discontent was instantly gone, replaced by the beginnings of fear. Nonthinkers of all cultures fall into line when their security is threatened. The trick is to keep them there.

"I need to check the building." Carter shuffled through papers in the briefcase. "Where is your list of tenants?"

The guard lumbered around the desk and picked up a clipboard. He started to hand it over, then his broad face clouded with suspicion.

"And a list of employees," Carter added. "We'll be letting some go. Sorry."

The guard sucked in his breath and picked up another clipboard. Again he hesitated to hand the information over.

"You look as if you know your job," Carter said. "Get much trouble here?"

"From Lebanese mostly." The guard had wild black eyebrows that were knitting in puzzlement as he considered the Westerner who spoke Arabic like a native. "I can't show these to just anybody."

"Call Aramco. They'll tell you. Where's your directory?"

Carter leaned over the desk as if to look. Instead, he memorized the number on the telephone. The guard started through the directory, looking up occasionally to mumble the alphabet. Carter nodded toward the lobby restrooms.

"Be right back," he said.

Once inside a tiled stall, Carter snapped open the briefcase and made minute adjustments on the fake recorder. Then he entered on its keyboard the lobby's telephone number.

"This is James Buchanan, vice-president in charge of

real estate for the Arabian American Oil Company.'' His voice was smooth, professional, his Arabic having a slight American accent.

"Sir!" the guard said.

Carter imagined the security guard standing up straight, at attention, at a call from an official of the oil company that had made Saudi Arabia—and, by example, other Arab countries—rich.

"Is my man there? Take good care of him. If you do, we won't forget you," Carter went on. "Employee loyalty is a major consideration in advancement at Aramco.''

It is astounding how reliable and trouble-free a little intimidation and bribery can be. A Killmaster learns to quickly assess when they should be used. An unscheduled killing can sometimes blow an assignment, and more information can be had from the living than from the dead.

When he came out of the restroom, the security guard couldn't do enough for Nick Carter.

The guard showed Carter the lists, went over them carefully, told stories about some of the people, hinted at questionable lifestyles and politics, and in the process Carter learned that the KGB agent he knew as Elena Markova was known to the guard as Ms. Leni Marks, a sales representative for a West German chemical company that made oil field supplies. She was gone frequently, had at least one Iraqi boyfriend, and lived in apartment 712B overlooking the river.

The Tigris River was rippled and green below Nick Carter. Iraqis in houseboats, *gufas*, and rowboats moved up and down it, shouting their wares to the patios of the expensive homes that lined the river. Date palms and poplars clustered artistically around the homes, part of their structural designs. Pedigreed dogs penned in formal flower gardens barked. Painted marble statues spouted water onto manicured front lawns with hedges that never varied in height by more than six millimeters. And through all this carefully displayed wealth spread the thick aroma of the river: hot, fishy, and decayed. Some things still cannot be bought.

Carter noted this as he made his way out a hallway window onto a narrow concrete balcony, and—rappelling—let himself down one story and over to the equally narrow balcony he knew to be outside the apartment of Elena Markova alias Leni Marks. The things that could not be bought, Carter thought as he peered around a fan palm on the balcony, are what make people and nature superior to any coin of the realm.

Then he grinned, wiped his face, and squatted. He didn't have to hurry.

On the other side of the sliding glass door on an immaculate white carpet lay Elena, fully dressed, beneath the panting young officer. While he yanked down her panties and opened his trousers, she gazed indifferently at the half-full cups of coffee on the slate coffee table and stroked his ear, her wine-red fingernails going around and around. Occasionally she remembered to nibble an earlobe.

The officer threw the lace panties across the room, shouted, and pounced on her, a tiger ready to relieve his lady in heat.

Carter put away his rappelling equipment and got out the striated tape. While Elena was fascinated by the coffee cups, he would do a little work.

He cut four three-inch strips of tape and attached them, a solid square, to the glass beside the lock on the door. Elena was looking at her watch and petting the soldier's head. The tiger came in five easy strokes. By taking care of his own needs, he assumed he was taking care of the lady's, too. Ineptness is everywhere.

Carter rubbed his thumbnail over the striations. Heat and ozone struck his nostrils. Elena was staring patiently at the ceiling. The officer's eyes were closed. He was grinning and had begun to talk. Carter unlocked the sliding glass door through the hole he'd silently made and eased it open.

"My colonel is happy that you will convert, little one," the young officer said, smiling. He had a distinctive, nasal voice. "He tolerates our liaison, you know, only because of his great vision. The more People of Purity, the better, is his thought. Another colonel would have you stoned and me beheaded.''

"You are worth any risk," Elena cooed, still petting his head. "When I become a Shiite, what do I expect?"

"Me. I will always take care of you.'' He rolled off to lie beside her on the white carpeting. He tucked her blond head against his shoulder.

"A woman needs a man's protection," Elena offered.

"Yes."

"Just as the Arab world needs the colonel."

"Most definitely, yes."

"Is that why the headquarters are so busy these days?" Elena propped her chin on the Iraqi's chest and stared into his eyes.

He ran his finger down her nose and across her lips.

"Don't bother your pretty head."

"Why did he go to Saudi Arabia in disguise?"

"I will be safe, little one. Don't worry. The colonel knows God, and now the people are beginning to know the colonel," he said in his nasal tones, proudly. "He is more and more popular, and he won't waste the opportunities it gives him."

"What is he planning?" Elena's voice had an edge to it. She was growing exasperated.

"Why," the young officer said, surprised, "what we have always planned. It is our duty to convince others that Muhammad passed the rule to his daughter Fatima and her husband Ali. The Sunnite caliphs are imposters. You know the creed, 'There is no god but God and Muhammad is the messenger of God.' That's why we add 'and Ali is the chosen friend.' As soon as we get the rest of Islam on sound religious footing again, the entire world will pay attention to the wisdom of our ways. They will see that they should be chosen too."

"What do you mean by 'the rest of Islam'?"

"Iran, Saudi Arabia, Lebanon . . . you know."

Elena sighed. "I know." She shrugged, giving up this round with a boxer who didn't know the game, and jumped to her feet, laughing. "What a lover!" she exclaimed, tugging on his hands, giggling, as he got to his feet. "You've exhausted me! And look at my hair . . ." She shook her head, and curls fell across her sculpted face with the high cheekbones. She was beautiful. "A mess! And I must still see clients today!"

He tried to put his arms around her, but she escaped, still laughing, then helped him straighten his uniform. She led him to the door, and they lingered there, his eyes heavy-lidded with success and the knowledge of future triumphs. She kissed him deeply before she closed the door.

And then she really laughed, loud, her back against the closed door. Laughed at the man who was fool enough to think he could ever satisfy Elena Markova. He was a lout who fucked but who would never know how to make love. When she had finished and wiped her eyes almost as if she had been crying, she adjusted her dress and walked to the coffee table. She bent to pick up the cups that needed washing . . .

And stepped to the glass door.

Her hand held an automatic that came straight through the opening, millimeters from Nick Carter's nose.

He blinked once, Hugo in his hand.

"I suggest you come inside," Elena Markova said in Arabic. "It's so much easier to talk, don't you agree?"

Carter nodded and Elena opened the door, backing away, a 9mm Parabellum steady in her hand. She knew how to hold a gun and she knew how to deceive, and Carter respected her for both. He walked into the room, not particularly concerned. It was little loss, and he might learn more this way.

"I should've known I couldn't fool you, Elena," he said in Russian.

She was a tall woman, Elena, in her rumpled blue dress and gold hoop earrings. Her shoes were gone, and her dress clung to the sweat on her curves. Her lips seemed swollen, almost bruised, the remnants of a sexual frustration she would never admit. For her, it was part of the job.

"And I should've known you would follow me, N3,"

she said good-naturedly in English.

Life is not tidy and well organized. A survivor learns to be flexible, to flow with life's changing currents and to keep his head afloat. A Killmaster learns more—to swim with, against, and across the currents, intelligently gambling his survival skills against the success of the moment. Carter felt Hugo in his hand, but he wanted to talk.

Elena's automatic was in the air before she could react, sailing from Carter's kick into a cut-glass chandelier above an ivory-inlaid dining room table.

Glass crashed and sprayed.

Carter spun away and pulled out Wilhelmina.

As he came around, Elena countered with an expertly placed kick to Carter's chin that sent him sprawling onto the white carpet. Wilhelmina skidded out onto the narrow balcony.

Carter grabbed Elena's ankle and flipped her onto her back.

He jumped up and so did she.

They stood there a moment, unarmed. Then they began to circle each other, looking for an opening.

Phillips closed his eyes and imagined picking up the radio and heaving it out the door. He saw it crash into a thick ebony tree and shatter, wires like disemboweled intestines dropping over leaves and grass, and he smiled, a slow smile that filled him with anticipation.

This time he got through.

"Yes, comrade?" The voice had the dull tones of the professionally polite.

"When are you jerks going to get equipment that works?" Phillips snarled. "Either your lines go dead or they get crossed and I end up talking to some idiot in Russky public relations. Public relations! You're wasting my time!"

There was a sharp intake of breath from the trained bureaucrat in Moscow.

"Patience is the—" the radioman tried.

"Screw patience! I want to talk to Blenkochev!"

"I'm sorry, comrade," the voice said coolly now. "We have no one here by that name. Perhaps it *is* public relations that you want?" The sneer was in the tone, not in the words, a coward's revenge.

Phillips grinned. "Get me 735-KB5-4398, you bastard. And hurry. Blenkochev will have your badge!"

Phillips listened with satisfaction as the radioman's earphones dropped. He sat back on the campstool and rubbed his hands. Money. That's what he needed—more money. He'd never have enough. He'd eaten plaster and boiled rats and drunk gutter water to fill his belly when he was a kid. He'd got used to it. No money; no choice. He squeezed his upper arms and felt the muscles hard and flat against bone. Maybe it had been good for him. Made him tough. Made him not expect anything from a world where creeps chased—

"KB5," Blenkochev said irritably, "your orders are to report only to KA2 in Khartoum."

"You have the imagination of a gorilla, Blenkochev. Also the face."

The radio was silent.

"Blenkochev?"

"I'm a businessman, KB5. Don't push. You have a limited shelf life as it is. What did you do—sharpen your fangs on Hawk first?"

"Maybe."

"No matter. You have precisely thirty seconds to empty your brain. That should be more than enough time, considering its paltry size."

"It'll cost you."

"Of course. What did Hawk pay?"

"Twenty thousand American."

"Four thousand, then, Not a ruble more."

"What?"

"Be sensible, KB5. Why should I pay for used information? So that I can keep up with Hawk? Nonsense. If it's really big, I'll hear through channels. AXE is a bureaucracy like any other. It eats time like an elephant eats peanuts. By the time they've geared up to do anything, we'll either hear from one of our agents in the field or from one of our moles in Washington. If I pay you anything for this at all, you're damned lucky. Next time, come to me first. After all, that was our agreement.''

"Don't pout, Blenkochev. It doesn't suit you. Seventy-five hundred and you've got a deal.''

"Very well. Just this once, and to remind you that the KGB keeps its agreements and you would do well to do the same . . . five thousand.''

"Done. Credit it to my Swiss account in twenty-four hours. If you don't, then I'll—''

"Threats are a waste of time with me, KB5. And they're unprofessional and tiresome as well.''

"Afraid I might scare you?''

Blenkochev laughed. "Dammit, KB5. Get on with it. What's this great information Hawk paid you ten thousand for?''

"How'd you—''

". . . know that it was ten? I didn't. Don't forget I got to be a businessman by first being an agent—an entry-level position, I think you call it. Now on with it. No information, no money. And maybe no money even then.''

It was Phillips's turn to laugh. "You're just like me. No wonder I don't offend you.''

"Much.''

Now they both laughed, and Phillips told Blenkochev about Major General Gamal Farouk, chief of the Egyptian secret police, and the scrap of paper with the words "Day of the Mahdi" and "Nyala.''

As he talked, Phillips continued to smile, his thin body relaxed on the campstool. He'd made another sale, for the pay he'd expected, and he knew that Blenkochev would remember to pay because Phillips's services were valuable. Blenkochev was a very good businessman.

SIX

Elena Markova's face was smooth against the afternoon sun, slipping in and out of the shadows of the room, around and around with Nick Carter, her flowing movements that of a cagey feline on the prowl.

Carter watched for an opening.

Elena's eyes calculated distances and risks.

"It's been a long time, Nick," she purred, but her face was sharp and watchful beneath the soft, creamy skin.

"Too long," Carter agreed, smelling the scents of perfumed woman and the oiled revolver that had been in her hand.

Their steps were slow, measured, as they made their circle.

"I've missed you, Nick," she said and smiled.

And she lashed out, her right hand hard and flat as a knife, at Carter's throat.

He parried, knocking the hand away, his blow sending Elena into a spin against the dining room table. She picked up a chair, legs out against Carter as if she were now a lion tamer and he a dangerous beast out of control. He swung against the chair and she almost lost it, recovering with renewed energy to use the chair to maneuver him against the wall.

He threw up his hands, exploding the chair into splinters that sailed across the room. She knotted her hands and smashed them down toward his neck. He ducked just in time, and her blow slid off him and onto a telephone table that shattered into ragged pieces around the four spindle legs. The receiver skidded away from the telephone, which instantly issued a piercing, continuous complaint.

She glanced at the telephone.

It was just a glance, but that was all Carter needed.

He bent over into her hips and stood up with her over his shoulder, his arm across her wiggling ass. She beat his back.

"Dammit, Nick!"

"I've missed you, too." He grinned and carried her through a likely looking door.

"Hurry up!"

Inside was a king-size bed, and he dumped Elena onto it. Her dress was a mushroom cloud above her waist, and she still didn't have any panties on. Carter stood over her. She made no effort to pull down the dress. Instead, she grabbed his wrist and yanked him down onto the bed between her legs. He kissed the swollen, frustrated lips that were like a hungry animal's, and she devoured his face, his neck, his shoulders, his chest . . . down, down, down.

He entered her slowly.

He stared into her eyes; she stared into his.

They made love, over and over, until at last the pain in her eyes was replaced by a deep glow, and the perpetual tightness in his back had disappeared into a distant memory.

They lay spent in each other's arms, their clothes in piles on the floor. Her naked body was warm and slippery with sweat and contentment beside him.

They slept.

When Carter opened his eyes, the bedroom was dim, the afternoon sun dying quickly into night. In the room was a long red dresser, two wingback chairs on either side of a reading table that held a brass lamp but no books, and night tables on both sides of the bed, again with brass lamps, although much smaller, and no books. The room had the feel of antiseptic cleanliness, like a hospital or motel room, as if people passed through but never stayed long enough to give it a sense of home or personality.

"You're awake." Elena ran a finger down his cheek. "I didn't know how much I'd missed you."

"Every few years, Elena."

"There's no one like you, Nick."

"I'm glad." He swept the moist hair from her face. "I wonder that you're so unchanged by it all. Still so beautiful. Even innocent."

She smiled. "They're all such damn fools."

"Men?"

"Men and women. Those who think they have the answers. It makes them vulnerable because they close their eyes. If you have the answers, why look?"

They spoke in German, the precise language of Schopenhauer, Hegel, and Goethe. Slipping from language to language was automatic for Carter. He often thought or dreamed in a variety of languages and had done this for so long that he was no longer amazed by it.

"I thought the KGB had the answers," he teased, pulling a silky strand of golden hair across his neck.

"Pretense. It's all pretense. They hope they have the answers."

"And you've got to believe as much as you can, or you couldn't do the work."

"I couldn't be an agent if I didn't believe in Mother Russia."

"And so you keep your innocence," Carter said.

He propped himself on an elbow so he could admire the slim hips, narrow waist, and round breasts beneath him. It was a young woman's body without the sag and stretch lines that came with age, yet he knew Elena to be in her mid-thirties. The body, the smooth face, and the dazzling style originated from an internal youthful innocence.

"The KGB's perpetual virgin," he said, holding her chin, staring at her.

Elena smiled, a slow smile that spread across her face like sunshine from behind a moving cloud. The frustration was gone, and the face was peaceful.

"I remember when I was a little girl," she said, "my

mother often took me to visit Lenin's tomb in Red Square. I'm from Moscow. I told you that before, didn't I?''

Carter nodded, stroking her chin.

''Yes,'' she said, ''I remember, too. Anyway, to the right in the square as we walked was the stone wall of the Kremlin, seventy feet high in places, and to the left was the Cathedral of Saint Basil with its onion domes. Mother would be holding my hand tightly, not because she was afraid of losing me in the crowds, but because she was so excited. She always smelled wonderful, of cinnamon and flour. She was a baker's assistant, you know.'' Elena smiled across the room as if it were a continent. ''Mother would walk right up to that wall and stop. She'd look it up and down, and then she'd point with her mitten. 'See this?' she'd say and shake the mitten. 'See this insulting high wall? It was built to keep you and me out. Palaces, cathedrals, monuments, riches to buy the world . . . all that on the other side. Before the Revolution, people like us never got in. We couldn't walk through the gates any time we wanted. Monarchists! Imperialists!' She'd spit on the ground. 'Comrades should stand out here and look at this disgusting wall and remember to be grateful.' After we stared at the wall some more, Mother would take me over to the tomb to see Lenin. We'd stand by the glass and this time Mother would cry. She'd cry and call him 'Papa.' She felt that way about him even though she was only a baby when the Revolution happened.''

Carter spread her blond hair out against the pillow.

''You don't think Lenin had the answers?'' he said.

''Some. What struck me about that wall wasn't just that it was built to keep people out. It was also built to keep people from seeing what they were being denied. It was a double loss.'' Elena turned to gaze thoughtfully into Carter's eyes. ''Why are you here? Why have you followed al-Barzani?''

''I was going to ask you the same question,'' Carter replied.

''We are a pair, aren't we?''

''You keep looking over fences to know whether what's on the other side is worth going after.''

"My job," she said simply. "Yours, too."

"There's not much I can tell you," he said.

"Even if you could," she finished his thought. "I could tell you that my company's pleased with the new oil clients I've gotten them. That I'll get a bonus, a Mercedes 380, and a company-paid vacation on Majorca."

"You're lucky to get to Gdansk," Carter said and laughed.

"It's better than Pittsburgh," she retorted, and then she laughed, too.

"What were you doing in Pittsburgh?"

She twined a finger slowly through the hair on his chest and looked up coquettishly. "Would you really like to know?"

Carter watched her for a moment, then shook his head. "You've never been to Pittsburgh."

"Ah, Killmaster!" she hooted. "Master spy! Agent extraordinaire! Your powers of observation astound me!"

She had wide blue eyes that complemented the blond hair. Scandinavian eyes that were deep-set as if perpetually watching sunrise or sunset. When she laughed, the skin around them crinkled into filigreed webs, and her soft female body curled around him. Now she smelled of perfume and sex.

"Shut up." Carter kissed her deeply, his tongue feeling the sudden moistness in her mouth. She rose to meet him, surprised and eager, as he pulled up her legs and spread them.

Afterward they lay entwined. His breathing was hard and good. She panted lightly.

"Oh, God," she murmured. "Only with you, Nick. It only works this good with you."

"You're a strange woman, Elena," he said. "You could have anyone you wanted. Yet you want your work more than you want any man."

She shrugged. "You could have any woman you wanted. You're the same."

"Our brand of permanence."

"Every few years . . ." She pulled his face around

and kissed him. She fell back against the pillow, thinking.

He felt her arm, the muscles beneath the velvet skin. She probably kept a set of weights in one of the apartment closets.

"Nick . . . do you know a man named Melvin J. Cooley?"

"American?"

"Uh-huh. High-ranking businessman. Chairman of the board of Universal Mining and Refining Company."

"Don't know the man, but UMRC is a giant holding company. Rates near the top of the Fortune 500. You run into Cooley here?"

"Sort of. No formal introductions. It's puzzling. UMRC has no business dealings in Iraq, yet I've seen one of al-Barzani's aides talking with Cooley secretly in the file room. Why would a medium-rank Iraqi soldier command Cooley's attention? And then, later, al-Barzani himself and Cooley met casually but obviously intentionally and had another long, secret conversation . . . this time in the men's john."

"The men's john? How—"

She groaned in mock horror. "Don't ask. It's a long story."

"Probably through the window."

She looked at him in surprise. "It was an old-fashioned transom—"

"And you were suspicious." He touched the end of her nose. "You almost got caught."

"Can't figure out what he's doing here."

"Sounds as if you can't figure out what al-Barzani's up to either."

Her face closed as completely as if a curtain had dropped before it.

"Maybe," she said.

"I'm not doing any better," he said conversationally. "Al-Barzani's a fascinating man. A lot of potential trouble there. Makes me wonder what he was doing in Saudi Arabia. Shiite Muslims are third-class citizens there. Is he trying to organize them?"

He had given her some of his speculation, not a lot, but more than he would give anyone else. But then Elena had told him about Cooley, and that might turn out to be even more useful.

"Or convert them. I heard a rumor while I was there. One of the king's brothers is a Shiite now. No one in the royal family is supposed to know."

Carter stared at her. "Mujahid."

"Prince Mujahid," she confirmed, staring back.

As they looked at one another they were each asking the same question with their eyes. Had al-Barzani met with Mujahid?

"There were some places I couldn't go where they might have met," she said. "No females."

"I understand."

"Damn."

Most of the time, Nick Carter and Elena Markova were on opposite sides of an assignment. It was understandable. AXE and the KGB had similar but not compatible goals: leverage through foreign governments friendly to their respective nations. Few foreign governments that wanted financial, administrative, and materiel aid could maintain equal friendships with the Soviet Union and the United States for very long. It was only a matter of time until the governments slid to one side or the other, and it was AXE's and the KGB's job to make sure they slid to the correct side.

As Carter awoke, he was acutely aware that he was sleeping with the enemy.

He moved his head enough that he could see her soft female features in the streaming light of the full moon through the apartment window. Her lips were slightly parted. With the corner of the sheet, he dabbed her cheek and chin. She moved slightly, as if in annoyance, but then she smiled, and he knew she was dreaming. Perhaps of Moscow and her mother. For a moment he held his breath, caught by the vulnerability of the sleeping woman.

Then, moving with the stealth of the trained hunter, he

arose from the bed and dressed. She sighed, still deep in sleep, her hair a gold and silver halo against the pillow in the moonlight.

Some day, when they were on opposite sides of an assignment, he would have to kill her. Or she would kill him.

Life, after all, was occasionally very simple. Kill or be killed.

He picked up his briefcase and left, closing her apartment door silently behind him. He walked down the hall to the elevator, punched the button, and kicked the wooden door. Hard. He looked down at the hole he'd made in the door.

SEVEN

"*As-Salaam alaykum*," Carter told the Turkoman-dressed security guard as he came off the elevator.

"And upon you, peace," the security guard responded eagerly. He came from behind the lobby desk carrying clipboards. "In what other ways may I serve you, sir?"

"Just one more minor thing," Carter said. "By the way, Vice-President Buchanan will hear about your efficiency and loyalty."

Those were the magic words, efficiency and loyalty. The security guard beamed.

Carter held up the briefcase, patted its leather side.

"I'd like a quiet place to work on my report." Carter looked around the lobby.

"Anywhere, sir. Wherever you'd like."

"Perhaps in the office there? Does it have good light?"

"Oh, yes. Very good light. Let me show you."

The guard hurried to the door marked "Office," opened it, and switched on overhead lights hidden behind shutterlike boxes. The mahogany desk had a fresh coat of wax and gleamed in the soft lights. The desk was to the right of the door. No one sitting at it could be seen through the open doorway. Perfect. The guard turned on the brass lamp on the desk. The lamp was a replica of a Sumerian statue, probably dating from about 2300 B.C. The guard pulled out a new blotter from the top drawer and put it on the desk.

"For your papers, sir."

Against the opposite wall, a hand-knotted rug hung

from the ceiling. Cheetahs, gazelles, antelopes, and jerboas were caught in the rich threading as they ran through forests and across Iraqi plains. The floor was a black-and-white checked design formed by marble tiles. There was a two-drawer filing cabinet, mahogany, matching the desk, and on top of it was a tray with papers propped upright between two hand-carved ebony bookends. From where he stood, Carter read the title of the first paper: "Lease Agreement."

Carter sat at the desk and put his briefcase squarely on the blotter. He leaned back in the chair. It didn't creak. He adjusted his cuffs.

"This will do nicely," Carter said. "I'll leave the door open."

"Oh, yes. Of course, sir." The guard moved worriedly away. "I haven't offended . . . I mean, you're not concerned . . . ?"

"I want the door open only for the air circulation." Carter lifted the lid of his briefcase, then lowered it over his hand. He stared pointedly at the guard.

The security guard bowed low in his Turkoman hat and, clasping the clipboards to his enormous chest, scurried back to the lobby.

Carter moved silently to just behind the office door and squatted out of sight. He watched the lobby through the crack. The security guard was sitting at his desk, his profile silhouetted as he stared out into the night.

Carter didn't have to wait long.

Within fifteen minutes, Elena came swinging out of the elevator and across the lobby toward the street. She had on an evening suit of pearl gray silk. She was fresh, polished, and immaculate, showing no sign of their afternoon of sex. She must have jumped out of bed as soon as Carter had left.

She gave the security guard a dazzling smile. He brightened. It would make his day. Then she was gone, down the street past the lobby windows, her head held high and haughty.

● ● ●

Carter tailed Elena Markova through Baghdad's night. Crippled beggars clutched at his hands. Street children with dirty faces and old eyes held up their palms and patted empty, swollen bellies. Iraqi women in short, revealing Western dresses called to him, promising the traditional good time. The air was thick and turgid with the slow-moving night. Carter sweated as he followed the KGB agent.

Elena ignored the pleas of the street people. She kept up a steady pace, doubling back on sidewalks, crossing against lights, going into all-night tourist cafés and exiting out the backs into dark alleyways.

An amateur tailing someone tends to follow too closely. He is quickly discovered. After that, he will follow at too great a distance. By one quick step into a doorway or a shadow, the subject will lose him.

An expert sleuth knows that a moderate distance and a quick, anticipatory mind are the two keys to successful tailing.

Neither too close nor too far away, the distance in constant adjustment so that even the suspicious subject is kept off-balance. The anticipatory expert watches not only the subject, but where he or she might go. He observes idiosyncratic signals such as shoulder dips, hesitations, or a telling break in stride. Eventually he will know enough through observation to predict most of the subject's moves.

Elena Markova would have spotted and lost even an expert long ago.

But Nick Carter was a Killmaster, and he knew her. He watched her precautions with amusement. About twenty minutes earlier he had begun to suspect her destination. Now, as he walked across the street from her, back a hundred paces, he was sure.

He took off his suit jacket and folded it into his briefcase. Then, while still wearing it, he rebuttoned his specially designed white shirt, pulling out slip-sewn darts, to make a doctor's hospital smock. He rubbed on dark makeup as he walked unnoticed among the other freaks of

Baghdad. Last, he put on horn-rimmed glasses.

His appearance was that of the new breed of Muslim intern. Now the poor noticed him again with renewed pleas for help. He passed out coins on a street corner, watching Elena still walking a few doors south. If he was right, she wouldn't go much farther.

Beggars and urchins and slack-jawed women pressed around Carter, pulled at his clothes and hands, tried to get into his pockets, tugged at his briefcase.

Well-dressed Iraqis smelling of toilet water and seasoned meats glared or averted their eyes in silent disapproval of the growing, foul-smelling throng that was eagerly palming the coins Carter gave them. Carter shrank down. He could see out through the chinks between arms and bodies and craning heads, but Elena would not be able to see in.

Elena Markova crossed once more, away from the destination he had thought for her. Her eyes moved. Her head turned slowly, observing all those who walked and stood along the street ripe with the odors of the Tigris.

Carter handed out his last coin. The crowd swelled indignantly, complaining and restless.

Elena studied the crowd from her distance, took a questioning step toward them.

Carter dug in his pockets and handed out, one at a time, small bills. A murmur of approval ran through the crowd like a shiver through a corpse. Even the dead like to live a little. They towered over him.

Elena changed her mind. She crossed the street again and, swinging her pocketbook, walked directly where Carter had predicted—into al-Barzani's headquarters. She walked as if she owned the whole block.

EIGHT

The two soldiers who stood in their perfect uniforms at the door to al-Barzani's headquarters did not officially acknowledge Elena Markova, but their eyes followed her swaying hips as she walked through the entryway and down a hall lit by overhead fluorescent lights.

The crowd walked with Carter toward the headquarters, smiling their toothless smiles as he batted their hands from his pockets.

"No more!" he said in the street's broken dialect. "No more! Sorry!"

They tore at his clothes and cried and shouted. He threw his last small bills into the air and strode into the black shadow of the building directly across the street from the headquarters.

He lit a cigarette as the urchins and beggars scrambled on the sidewalk for what the comfortable would consider only coffee money. It made him ashamed of himself and the world.

He inhaled deeply on his cigarette and forced his gaze away to examine al-Barzani's headquarters. To make a better world, he had his own work to do. He wasn't a social worker.

Al-Barzani's headquarters was a four-story narrow brick building with a central hall running down the middle of each floor. Elena came into view again on the third floor. She tapped on a door near the front and went in. Carter walked down the sidewalk and counted windows on the building. He ground out his cigarette and dropped the butt into his pocket.

The street people were back to their regular stations. They no longer showed any interest in him.

He looked up, gazed a moment at the night's arrangement of stars, then stalked across the street to the headquarters.

"There is no god but God, and Muhammad is the messenger of God," Carter said in Arabic, watching the two soldiers standing guard smile as he went on without hesitation, "and Ali is the chosen friend."

"Greetings, brother," the older one said. "If there's someone sick nearby, I'll pray for him."

"The world is sick," Carter said, "sick and evil."

The two soldiers nodded. They were in their early twenties with black cotton beards and ingenuous eyes. The younger had a rash of pimples on his forehead.

"I saw a woman with Western ways come in here." Carter's voice dropped into a sneer when he said the word "woman." "I thought more of you, of Colonel al-Barzani. What's to become of the People of Purity when you consort with a shameless hussy?" His voice dripped disgust and piousness. "And Colonel al-Barzani wants to be our leader!"

The young soldiers were in agony.

". . . great leader!" the younger sputtered.

"He's a scholar of the Koran!" argued the other. "He lives without sin!"

"If you could only hear him explain . . ."

Carter crossed his arms. "I hear no explanations. Only excuses. My colleagues at the hospital have had respect for al-Barzani's positions, but now when I tell them this . . . and I *must* tell them . . ."

Conviction is important. Without conviction, nothing would be accomplished—no acts of heroism, no great music, no daring inventions, no thriving cities. But conviction has another side for those who are not original thinkers. It is the side of insecurity. Nonthinkers want everyone to believe what they believe to ensure their correctness.

"No!" exclaimed the older.

"The colonel will explain!" said the younger, his pimples glowing red.

"I don't have time to talk to the colonel," Carter said, tapping his briefcase and stepping away. "I'm on a call. I stopped only because I saw that . . . that"—his voice rose—"that *unveiled woman . . .* !"

The soldiers grabbed his arms. The older gave him directions to al-Barzani's office on the fourth floor with apologies that they couldn't go with him because they had to stay at the door.

They pushed him down the hall, and he went, feet dragging, until he disappeared up the staircase where he could speed his way to the third floor. He passed other Zab Brigade soldiers and officers, and they nodded to him without curiosity. The guards on duty at the door, although young, were trusted. Probably the building and its purpose were well known enough that they received the support—and perhaps even the surveillance—of the neighborhood.

Carter stopped outside the door Elena had entered.

The hall was empty, but it wouldn't be for long. He took out Wilhelmina and held it under the smock pocket. Beyond the door he heard the tones but not the words of Elena Markova.

He walked down the hall to the next door. Behind it, a telephone rang and was interrupted by a hearty male answer. Carter backtracked to the office on the other side of where he could still hear Elena talking to someone. The crack beneath the door of this office was dark. He heard nothing from inside.

He twisted the doorknob of the dark office, pushed open the door, and slid noiselessly inside against the wall.

The room was as quiet as it was dark. Carter moved to the wall it shared with the office Elena was in. He felt his way along it until he came to an inner door. The knob turned easily, and he opened it enough to hear not only Elena's voice, but also the distinctive nasal tones of her officer lover.

"Nick Carter," she said, exasperated. "He undoubtedly followed me."

"But I don't understand," the officer said.

Carter imagined him with his hands turned up, puzzled.

"It isn't necessary that you understand," Elena said. "It *is* necessary—"

"But how can he hurt us?" he interrupted. "No one can hurt us. We will prevail."

"Oh, God," Elena said tiredly. "At *what* will you prevail? What are the colonel's plans?"

"The colonel will command legions."

"Are you as much a fool as you sound?" Elena was openly disgusted. Her voice was sharp, as if instructing a young child. "The Brigade is getting ready for a big operation. More and more supplies are coming in and immediately routed off. There are secret, mid-week practice maneuvers. Recruiters are bringing in new men. The safe upstairs is full of cash. What does that sound like to you?"

The only sound in the room was the heavy footsteps of the officer as he paced.

"It sounds as if you're more interested in our operations than you are in me." His nasal voice was cold. His speech pattern had the crispness of intelligence. Elena hadn't been the only one playing games.

"My, my," she said. "Not so simple, are you, my darling?"

The telephone was picked up, the officer's voice official, "An enemy agent may be in the building. Question the guards about strangers of any kind, and begin an immediate search."

"What a man," Markova cooed. "My clever man."

"What does Carter know?" the officer said harshly.

"He doesn't know I know who he is, for one thing. He does know the colonel was in Riyadh the last few days. If that's true. Does Carter know what he's talking about, darling?"

"That's none of your business." The officer was still stern, but he was weakening. "What else did he say?"

"That he saw Prince Mujahid and the colonel together,

and that they have agreed to be military allies.''

Silence.

A desk moving.

"Oh, my lover," Elena said tenderly. "You are the best . . . ahhh . . ."

The knock at the officer's door was firm and impatient.

"What!" shouted the officer.

"This is Cooley." The voice was full, deep, jovial, with a hint of the U.S. South in the halting Arabic. "I hope you're workin' and not doin' what I think you're doin', Lieutenant."

More movement inside the room.

People and furniture.

A door opening.

"Well, well, Lieutenant," Cooley said heartily. "Can't say as how I blame you. Who's this pretty miss . . . no, no, never mind. Name's Honey, I'll bet. All you girls're named Honey, ain't that right?"

Carter imagined Elena's sweetly smiling face as she repressed scathing comments to the ignorant rich man who used humor to make good manners of his hatreds.

"Leni Marks," Elena said in her best cultured voice.

"She's a sales representative for DeutsChem," the lieutenant said. "She's gone so far over her quota that she's won a Mercedes."

Cooley hooted. "She tell you that? You're a sucker, boy. She's got some big daddy buyin' her all the lollipops she wants. You're a diversion. For a . . . *lady* . . . like this, you'll never be more than a diversion."

"Mr. Cooley," Elena said, her Arabic impeccable. "I'm delighted to meet you at last. You're the man to be congratulated for UMRC's growth." She switched to the honeyed English of the Deep South. "I remember when I was at the University of Virginia, you bought out South Atlantic Refining and added it to UMRC's portfolio. That was quite a coup."

"You were a student in Charlottesville?"

"German exchange student. Economics."

"Economics. You don't say."

"My Leni is remarkable," the lieutenant said in

Arabic. He was uncertain of the conversation, but the course was unmistakable.

"Thank you, darling," Elena said sweetly. "We're engaged, Mr. Cooley. I hope you'll be able to come to the wedding."

Cooley gave a rueful laugh. "The joke's on me. My apologies, Miss Marks," he said in English. "Guess the old eyes've seen too many jigaboos in the last two weeks. What a country."

Bigots are the same around the world. They facilely shift from one hatred to another.

"I understand, Mr. Cooley," Elena said in Arabic. "I'm surprised to see such an important man as you in Baghdad."

"Can't send a scout to negotiate an important deal," Cooley said.

"Please, Mr. Cooley," the lieutenant said, "this is of the utmost secrecy."

Cooley's hearty voice was back on comfortable ground.

"She's one of the family now," he said. "If you can't trust her, then you'd damn well better not marry her."

"Of course he trusts me," Elena said. "Don't you, darling?"

There was hesitation in darling's voice.

"Well, Leni," he said slowly, "it's not that I don't trust you . . ."

Footsteps sounded in the hallway. There were several soldiers. They had the easy rhythm of those who walked great distances. Carter balanced Wilhelmina in his hand.

"Come, come, boy. Make a decision. I've got to talk to you about this Mahdi business. Either send her away, or let's get on with it."

The footsteps had stopped outside the hallway door.

Carter crept silently to the window. Soldiers stood below, staring up. Two of them were the youngsters from the front door. They looked angry . . . and betrayed.

A shot exploded the windowpane.

The door burst open.

NINE

With reflexes fast as a thought, Nick Carter ducked and rolled across the office floor back to the door where he had listened to Elena Markova's conversation with her boyfriend and Cooley.

The office's overhead lights flashed on.

Two dozen shots exploded into the wall and door behind Carter.

With Wilhelmina, Carter picked off three soldiers as they leaned into the door to take aim. Two he got through the heart, but the third he shot through the ear and the bullet blew the other ear off, splattering the faces of his comrades in the hall.

Carter kicked open the door behind him.

Bullets whizzed past him. He slammed the door shut.

They were a frieze—Elena, the lieutenant, and Melvin J. Cooley—in an unfinished three-way conversational cluster in the middle of a disheveled office. Elena's pearl gray evening suit was rumpled. The lieutenant's spit-and-polish uniform was askew, the belt not yet rebuckled, his tie off to one side. Melvin J. Cooley wore an immaculate white leisure suit beneath a face ravaged by fear.

The lieutenant grabbed his revolver off the desk.

Melvin J. Cooley—a lanky, tall, Southern gentleman with a shock of blond hair gone dirty gray at the temples and a belly that protruded like a basketball above toothpick legs—dropped to the floor and wrapped his arms around his head.

Elena glanced at Carter and then watched the lieutenant with interest.

57

With precision and no wasted motion, Carter kicked the revolver from the lieutenant's grip. He slashed a rock-hard hand into the lieutenant's stomach.

"Too slow, dear," Elena commented, smiling, to the lieutenant as he collapsed screaming over his belly.

Both doors into the lieutenant's office crashed open.

"Don't be shy, Elena," Carter said in German as he slid behind the lieutenant's desk. "You'll miss all the fun." Bullets whizzed over his head.

"Your party, dear," Elena said in German as she bent over to pat the lieutenant's shoulder in pretended commiseration. "Wish I could join the game," she said to Carter.

The lieutenant moaned, his arms locked over his belly. His face was blue because of the oxygen he had lost.

"What's going on?" Cooley shouted, his head buried in his arms against the floor. "Are you all crazy? Don't you know who I am?"

"Too well," Carter said in German as he shot through the doors.

"Much too well," Elena agreed, dragging the lieutenant to a wall away from the bullets.

Carter estimated there were twelve soldiers left, six at each door. The lieutenant's office provided little cover. Besides the desk, there were only three metal chairs—now peppered with bullet holes—and a map that covered one wall. The map was not just of Iraq, but of the whole Middle East. Strategy pins of different colors had been stuck in Iraq, Iran, Saudi Arabia, and the Sudan.

A bullet ripped through the corner of the desk, shooting wood splinters through Carter's white shirt-smock, burning into his side.

Soldiers suddenly poured in through the doors.

Carter quit firing.

"Sorry I can't stay," Elena shouted over the uproar of pounding feet and yelled orders. "I'd like to help!"

Her lieutenant had fainted at last, his head rolling to the side. She dragged him into the hallway. He was her ticket to whatever the big game was at al-Barzani's headquarters, and she wasn't going to lose him.

Cooley squirmed his way to the door. The soldiers avoided stepping on him. He looked like someone's overfed pet snake.

Al-Barzani's soldiers surrounded the three exposed sides of the desk. Their guns were high, their faces black with murderous intent.

They didn't shoot.

They wanted him alive.

Carter pulled out Pierre and hid him in his palm.

"Drop your weapon!" a sergeant ordered in Arabic.

"Where, sir?" Carter responded meekly. He stood up, looking bewildered. He held Wilhelmina pressed flat like a shield against the fast-spreading blood on his white shirt.

"Infidel!" the sergeant accused. "Hand it over!"

The soldiers looked scornfully at the man who had so little sense.

"Gladly."

Carter grinned and reversed Wilhelmina so he could hand her to the sergeant butt first. The soldiers were unaccustomed to such politeness. They stared at Carter's face.

Carter's grin widened as, with the remarkable skill and deceptiveness born of experience, he cracked Wilhelmina over the sergeant's skull.

The Luger's blow made a satisfying crunch that split the sergeant's parietal bone. The sergeant dropped.

The furious soldiers attacked.

Carter activated Pierre and released him to the floor, hissing. The small but potent gas bomb would go off in ten seconds. Not much time, even for a Killmaster.

In midair, Carter blocked a fist and twisted it one-handed, glancing at the soldier's shocked brown eyes as the fist snapped between the carpals and the radius and ulna, splitting bones to the shoulder.

He hit a belly with his elbow and knocked out a fine set of teeth with the flat of his hand. He kicked and spun through the mass of soldiers. The momentum carried him like a perpetual motion machine on an arc of broken necks and jaws and then out the body-strewn door, down the corridor, away from the immediacy of Pierre.

As Carter raced down the stairs, two slower-reflexed soldiers far behind, the bomb coughed into explosion.

There was sudden silence. Smoke gusted after Carter. The last two soldiers hadn't made it.

Wearing his disguise with new jauntiness, Carter gripped his bloody side with one hand, his briefcase with the other, and sauntered out the back of al-Barzani's headquarters into the stream of Baghdad's night.

Years ago, when the Saudi Arabian King Abdul Aziz was modernizing Arabia, he had trouble with the *ulamas*, the ultraconservative group of theologians who oversee the nation's religious life. So, to convince them that telephones would be desirable, he arranged for a call to be made to the learned teachers. It began with a recitation from the Koran. ''You cannot tell me,'' the king said to the august group afterward, ''that any instrument that can carry the word of God is an evil instrument.'' The telephones were installed.

Nick Carter reflected on this as he picked up the telephone in the modern booth on the west side of the Tigris. Battles are won in many ways. What is important is whether the result is worth the bother and, sometimes, the bloodshed.

He put a coin in the slot and dialed.

David Hawk, head of AXE, bit down on the soft sweet mass of his current cigar. Hawk's cigars had been particularly sweet that day. He knew his secretary didn't think so. She'd closed the door between their offices two hours ago. He'd hired Ginger Bateman because of glowing references and the fact that if she did smoke, she didn't smoke on the job. Nasty stench, cigarette smoke, not at all like the full, deep aroma of a good cigar.

He didn't like the sound of Carter's report. He was a good man, Carter, the best without question, but bad news even from Carter didn't sit well.

''No, drop the Beirut matter, N3,'' Hawk advised.

"That situation has a much longer fuse, despite the killings, and in the end will be less a problem than an entire Arab uprising."

"You think what I've got here might have that potential?"

"I'd rather have a thousand Beiruts," Hawk answered. "Religious fanatics have the strength of their beliefs behind them. They hate nonbelievers, and these fanatics stretch across a subcontinent of nonbelievers."

"I understand."

AXE's best agent had sense, Hawk knew. He figured Carter had probably come to the same conclusion about the information on his own, but Hawk had the tact not to say so.

"That why you didn't call in earlier?"

"I wanted to get all I could for you, sir," Carter said.

Hawk cleared his throat and puffed on the cigar. Damned good cigar.

"So, we've got Cecil Young's information about Prince Mujahid going into Riyadh," Hawk said almost to himself, "and that Mujahid may have switched camps to the Shiites. Then we've got Colonel al-Barzani, a devout Shiite Muslim, making a secret trip to Riyadh for unknown reasons." He pulled the cigar out of his mouth and stared at it. "You know what a Mahdi is, N3?"

"A messiah prophesied by some Islamic sects."

"Right. The Shiites believe that a Mahdi will come some day." Hawk set the cigar in the glass ashtray on his desk. The cigar had lost its flavor. "I got a call from an agent in the Sudan. Phillips. He found the chief of Egypt's secret police lost and unconscious on the White Nile. The guy had a message on him; most of the words were gone, but 'Day of the Mahdi' and 'Nyala' remained."

"Cooley mentioned a Mahdi," Carter said quickly. "Said he wanted to talk to the lieutenant about it."

"Anything else?"

"The Sudan. There was a map on the lieutenant's wall. Pins in Middle Eastern countries, including the Sudan."

"Nyala's in the Sudan."

"I know, sir."

Hawk picked up the cigar, rolling the familiar thickness between his thumb and fingers.

"Better get down there, Nick." He put the cigar in his mouth and chewed. "Cooley has no business in Iraq. Find out what's going on in the southern Sudan. And find that Egyptian."

TEN

Modern steel and glass buildings rise to tower above the traditional parapeted stone buildings of Baghdad. Carter walked beneath the darkened structures, looking for an inconspicuous café. Just as all cities have pollution they also have inconspicuous cafés. Part of contemporary worldwide culture. He found one with black glass windows and a door that rang a bell when opened. He was the only customer.

He ignored the waiter's stares at his bloody side and ordered black coffee, then walked through and around a corner to the restroom. Grease and heavy spices assaulted his nose from the nearby kitchen. He went into the restroom.

If he stopped to lean against the wall, he'd collapse. Exhaustion, not loss of blood. The only sleep he'd had in the past forty-eight hours had been in Elena Markova's bed, and that had hardly been restful. His last meal was on the flight to Baghdad. He smiled slightly, propped himself up against the washbasin, and stared at his haggard face in the mirror. Some Killmaster.

He splashed cold water on his face, then turned on the spigot full force and stuck his head into the refreshing water. Chills spread up his spine. Better already.

He took off his bloodied shirt and threw it in the wastebasket. A truly modern café to have a wastebasket and not just a pile of wadded cloths and papers in a corner.

He took two flat, foil-wrapped packages from his briefcase and opened them. He laid the antibiotic-treated gauze against his side. The gauze adhered like new skin. The cuts were small, the kind that bled out of all proportion to their seriousness, but untreated they could turn into a general infection that would slow him down.

He brushed his hair and rinsed his mouth. He again took out the black jumpsuit that he'd put on in the Riyadh airport and dressed in it. It would have to do for the flight to Khartoum.

He missed Pierre already, but he would be able to pick up more supplies in Khartoum. In order to be effective, AXE had to be everywhere, including Baghdad, but his Baghdad contact was across the city. The airport was closer. He'd get a taxi as soon as he had his coffee. If there was time, he'd have a big dinner in the airport before the flight took off.

He looked once more in the mirror, saw the familiar, strong face with the square jaw. He smiled. He no longer looked or felt haggard. Resilience and determination can compensate for just about anything.

He picked up the briefcase and opened the door. The smell of fresh hot coffee pleased him. Now he would think about the Sudan.

They were hiding behind the corner in the hall.

Four of them.

As one wrenched the briefcase from his hand, two others grabbed his arms and flipped him across the hall. He started to roll into a spring, but they threw their bodies across his arms to pin him down.

The fourth one laughed, his arms crossed as he observed. It was a nasty victor's laugh.

"Not so smart after all, Killmaster," the fourth said as he pointed a Luger at Carter's heart. He spoke good Midwestern English. Probably Iowa or Illinois.

The man with Carter's briefcase dropped it. He searched Carter, found Hugo.

"This is it, boss." He held up the stiletto. "He travels light." That one was probably from California.

"He travels cocky," the Midwestern leader said. "Tie him, then stand him up."

They put Carter on his feet, his arms tied against his sides and knotted to stay there with nautical rope that extended to skin-cutting loops around his thighs and calves. His side throbbed against the ropes.

"Trussed up like a pig," the Midwesterner commented as he looked Carter up and down. "Can't see what all the fuss is. Easy to catch as a catfish on a summer day."

The three others laughed at the boss's joke. They were dressed in Western polyester slacks, loafers, and open-necked shirts. They used deodorant. Lots of deodorant.

"Well, Killmaster," the Midwesterner urged, "speak up. I outsmarted you good and proper."

"Yup. You're smart," Carter drawled. "I know your kind. The only way you can count to twenty-one is to take all your clothes off."

The Midwesterner bashed Carter in the face. Carter's lip bled.

"Brave, too," Carter mused and licked his lip.

"Get him out of here!"

The three men picked up Carter and carried him through the café. Carter nodded to the wide-eyed waiter.

"Coffee smells good," he told him in Arabic. "I'll have that cup later."

"Like hell you will," the Midwesterner muttered as he followed the caravan out the door. The man knew Arabic. Carter raised his estimation.

They threw him in the back seat of a black limousine that was parked illegally at the curb. The Californian drove, the Midwesterner in the front seat beside him. The other two men sat on either side of Carter in the back seat.

"My horoscope said I could expect a trip," Carter said. "I didn't know it'd be at the expense of the CIA."

The Midwesterner wrenched around to stare at Carter, and the limousine took off down the street at breakneck speed.

"Shit," one of the men sitting next to Carter said.

"Goddamned independents," the other one said.

"AXE!" the Californian accused.

"We're supposed to be on the same side," Carter said.

"We're on the *right* side," the Midwestern leader said at last. "Agents like you make our jobs a pain."

"And we're not all CIA," the Californian said proudly as he twisted the wheel to dodge carts and pedestrians. "The good old U.S. Army can take some credit for putting you out of action."

"This is beginning to sound like a conspiracy," Carter said mildly. "Did you fellows learn independent thinking in high school? Ever consider that maybe someone's handing you a line of bull?"

The four Americans were determinedly silent after that, sitting in the smoothly running limousine that reeked of deodorant as it shot north through Baghdad's night.

Torture is from the Latin word *tortura*, which means twisting. The thought came quickly to Nick Carter's mind as he viewed the stone sewer that had been widened into an awkward room. In the center of it was a clumsily made rack. Three two-by-fours had been wired together into a ledge. On one end of the ledge were two more two-by-fours wired into an X and set in buckets of concrete. Wires stretched from the X to the foot of the ledge.

The two Americans from the back seat dropped Carter onto the ledge. The Californian cranked up a battery at the foot while the others tied Carter down.

"Nice little piece of hardware we picked up," the leader commented as he watched his men work.

It was a primitive rack, probably made by local artists, but it could snap a man's neck or pull off his testicles when the time came. First, the four Americans would have some fun.

Carter again felt chills go up and down his spine, chills that came from a very realistic fear.

"The President wouldn't approve of this," Carter said, looking around.

"Save yourself some grief, Carter," the Midwesterner said. "Tell us what we want to know."

"You ever do this before?" Carter asked. "It's a messy job, I hear. Enough to give a man nightmares for life."

"Don't worry about us," the Midwesterner chuckled. He had a flat face with eyes like a frog's, bulging out with anticipation. "Start with al-Barzani. What do you know?"

"Colonel in the Iraqi Army," Carter said. The important thing was to keep your mind on things other than your body and its future.

They wrapped wires around his ankles and across his chest beneath the armpits. The battery hummed into life, rotating a wheel-pulley system beneath the rack. His body stretched, held down at the shoulders; he concentrated on the open stream of brown sewage running down the center of the stone room.

"Hear a fellow can grow three inches this way," the Midwesterner said, watching. "What is al-Barzani up to?"

"Don't know," Carter said.

The wheel rotated.

The crack of Carter's joints reverberated over the quiet sound of the river.

Carter sweated.

"Did I mention that this battery will electrify the wires?" the Midwesterner asked innocently.

"Glad you thought of it," Carter said, sweat running down his forehead and burning his eyes.

The wheel turned.

Sharp pains shot through Carter's legs and into his chest. His back arched. He tried to focus his mind on the stench around him.

"Why are you in Baghdad?" the Midwesterner asked. "Please give us a bad answer." He smiled cruelly.

"Vacation," Carter said, his eyes closing at last in pain. He thought about the river, saw it running through his mind.

Still, he heard the wheel turn.

His clothes stuck to him in a sudden outpouring of sweat. His body swelled in red streaks of pain. His back was completely off the ledge, his legs stretched like rubber bands.

"Why do you want to know about Cooley?"

Carter grunted. He didn't want to grunt.

"Cooley! Why are you interested in Cooley?"

The men had pressed him too hard and too fast.

The pain turned black suddenly. A friend, black pain. Black as a void. Nothingness. All gone. Can't feel a thing. Unconscious.

As Phillips drew the launch up to the hospital compound in the Sudanese village, the natives scattered. He stalked across the hard-packed dirt without glancing after them, his hands resting casually on the Python revolvers holstered at his sides.

Cooking fires burned abandoned in front of the huts. The remains of the evening meal sat on bark and leaves. Thin, red-eyed dogs slunk up to the food, tails between their legs, sniffed, then wolfed the food.

The white hospital room was ablaze with the light from a half-dozen lanterns. The doctor's body was gone, but the rest of him still decorated the walls in a pink fading to brown.

The young Nilotic nurse backed away from the Egyptian, a stethoscope swinging from her neck. She froze against the wall, hands flat on it. Her eyes radiated naked fear. She was the same nurse as before.

Phillips grinned at her. She was a pretty thing in the way young Dinka natives can be. Thick-featured but soft, with the decorative scars of her tribe on her ebony skin. Probably had never had a Western man. Later, when he had time, he might take care of that.

Phillips stood over Major General Gamal Farouk, chief of the Egyptian secret police. Farouk didn't look good. His skin was gray, and he breathed heavily in whistling gusts.

"Haven't cleaned up here yet, I see," Phillips said conversationally in dialect. He pointed to the walls.

The Dinka girl shook her head. She trembled.

"Been too busy, I expect," he said.

The girl nodded. She had enormous eyes, black as coals.

"The Egyptian wake up yet?" he asked.

The girl licked her thick lips. "No."

"I need to talk to him," he said. "You understand, that was what the doctor and I disagreed about. Waking him up."

She nodded, the eyes now downcast.

"The doctor was a foolish man. I can see that you're not a man."

She looked up, her face stretching in horror and new fear.

It made him smile.

"And you don't look foolish, either," he said.

She stared at him, helpless as an urchin. She was the kind who'd be a wild animal in bed. She might actually be worth coming back to, for a short visit.

"I want you to help me wake him up."

She stared at her feet and shook her head.

"I insist."

"I don't know how. The doctor said it would kill him."

Phillips walked around the Egyptian to the girl. He cupped her round chin in his strong fingers. He lifted her face and squeezed the chin. Tears seeped out of the corners of her closed eyes.

"I really do insist."

She tried to shake her head.

He took out a revolver and pressed the barrel against her temple.

"Your stethoscope tells me you *do* know how. If you don't help me, I'll kill him . . . and you."

He felt the shudders of her terror in his hand. He was so close to her that the smell of woodsmoke and wild flowers in her hair was overwhelming. Her fear and odor made his chest contract, excited. He would come back. He shoved her against the wall and panted.

"You have no choice!"

There was a distant roar of jets, growing louder.

She continued to shake, lost in fear.

He dropped his hand and ran out the door to stand in the dirt compound, looking up.

Fighter jets, small and lethal, circled beneath the stars over the village. Phillips waited, watching, until at last a jet swooped lower and he saw the wings. The markings had been painted out.

ELEVEN

Carter awoke to blazing pain and a tuneless song. For a time, the excruciating pain eclipsed everything. At last the tuneless song filtered back into his consciousness. It sounded so far away it might have been in another country. He didn't try to look at the singer, nor even to open his eyes or change his breathing pattern. As long as his captors thought he was still unconscious, he could gather strength.

He didn't recognize the song and wondered whether the singer had something in mind for his singing other than killing time. The thought made him smile. He was feeling better.

It was time to assess the damage to his body.

Swollen. Sore. Exhausted. The impact of his throbbing side was now lessened by throbbing legs and back.

Using his mind as a probe, he began at his toes and worked his way up each leg. The joints still seemed connected, the bones unbroken. He tested his pelvis, then his back and chest. Nothing broken or snapped. The muscles sore, the flesh aching. No incapacitating damage. The CIA and the soldiers, for all their bravado, were inexpert at torture. Like anything else, too much pain can be ineffective. Although they hadn't pushed him to his mental limits, they had overwrought his body. It is the way with all humans. The mind is stronger than the body, but most people don't know that.

The singer quit. It was hard to tell whether it was a natural or an arbitrary finish.

Carter flexed his legs imperceptibly. Stabbing pain shot through him. It was tolerable pain. The wires around his ankles were still tight, but the wheel had been released. There was no tension to hold his body taut.

Were the CIA men and soldiers gone? Is that why the wheel had been released?

Carter resisted the impulse to open his eyes. A dead Killmaster was no use to anyone. A weakened Killmaster could get himself killed.

Always the mission first.

Carter concentrated now on his sense of hearing. Rats scrambled in a corner and down a wall. Far across the stone room, feet shuffled. The stinking river of sludge gurgled and murmured softly. Water dripped from the ceiling.

Carter flexed his legs again, working the circulation. Besides the wires around his ankles, he had wires wrapped across his chest and under his arms. His hands were wired down to the ledge of two-by-fours beneath him. He flexed his arms, stretched his neck, rippled the muscles across his back and chest. Slowly, the muscles began to respond.

The pain increased and then lessened.

Again Carter listened for the purposeful movements of guards. Nothing. He pulled against the wires, feeling for looseness and weakness. Sweat rolled off him, soaking into the boards beneath him. The wires were impossibly strong and tight. There was no way he could unwrap or break them.

He opened his eyes into slits. And grinned.

An old Arab with a grizzled beard and filthy rags was shuffling back and forth far across the room, making an erratic line marked by a trail of urine. The Arab wrung his hands and muttered to himself. The yellow streaks down the formerly white robes indicated that incontinence was part of the Arab's daily life.

"Greetings," Carter said in Arabic.

The old Arab jumped as if he'd been hit. He had a bulbous nose and sparse eyebrows, almost as if the eyebrows had been picked out in fits of nervousness. The Arab's eyes wavered around the room.

"Over here," Carter said.

The Arab drew his shoulders up to his neck and swiveled, a hand squeezing his groin. He stared at Carter and walked slowly toward him, the hand still on the groin. The trail of urine had stopped.

"Yes, master?" the old Arab said. His eyes never stopped moving, darting around the room fearfully, not once directly looking at Carter's face.

"I need you to help me," Carter said gently. "Will you unwrap these wires?"

"You don't like it here, master?"

"I do not. In fact, it's important that I leave."

"That would make the others very angry. Oh, my. Very angry." The old Arab's hands were palsied and shook at his side and on his groin. He licked his lips with a thick tongue and thought. "This is really a very nice place to be." The eyes kept moving. "You always know what's going to happen here. It is good to eliminate the uncertainties of life. Very good."

"I must leave. I'll pay you."

"I have everything I need," the old man said and turned away. "They take care of me." He began to sing the same tuneless song.

"What do you call what you're singing?" Carter called after him.

The old man looked over his shoulder. He stopped singing and turned servilely. The wrinkles on his face deepened in sadness.

"Anything you want to call it, master."

"There are hospitals that can help you."

The old Arab backed away, pursued by a demon.

"Knives! They'd cut it off!"

"Probably not. There are medicines. Small operations to tighten a valve."

"No!" The Arab raised his palsied hands in attack and urine again dribbled onto the stone floor. "No!" He ran at

Carter, his face contorted in unbearable fear.

"The University of Baghdad has a hospital," Carter continued. "I could take you. I'd pay."

The old man hesitated, his hands in mid-flight above Carter.

"You'd be the master," Carter said. "They'd do only what *you* told them."

The old man's mind worked over Carter's words.

"All you have to do is release me," Carter said softly.

The old man's heavy-lidded eyes blinked. The hands fell to the wire around Carter's neck and began to untangle it.

"No one should have to suffer," Carter said.

"*Abdul!*"

The Midwesterner's voice boomed like a cannon in the low-ceilinged room.

The old Arab jumped and grabbed his crotch.

The Midwesterner, his three followers, and two dozen Arabs with fierce faces swarmed through the archway, their leather-soled loafers and bare feet soundless on the stone floor.

The Californian picked up the old Arab by the back of his urine-streaked robes and swung him away into a heap in the corner.

"He was moving, master," the old man whined. "I didn't want him to get free."

"Gooks," the Midwesterner muttered and stared down at Carter. "Well, Killmaster, lucky for you you're still alive. Have a good sleep?"

"Passable."

"Back to work then."

The Arabs squatted in a circle around Carter, their knives dangling to the floor, their rifles across their laps. They grinned, waiting to be entertained. The Californian turned on the battery, tested the wires. The old Arab staggered to his feet and lurched toward the other Arabs, a hand shakily on his groin.

"Look, boss," one of the Americans said. "That old

bastard's playing with himself again.''

The Midwesterner shook his head, his thick lips curled in disgust below the frog eyes.

''Ought to be neutered, doing that in public,'' the Midwesterner commented.

The old man squatted unsteadily behind two Arabs. They moved together to block him from the circle. Carter pulled against the wires. Even Hugo wouldn't have been able to cut through.

''He is Allah's curse,'' said another.

''A dog on the street.''

It is not true that the slave dreams of being free. The slave doesn't know freedom; he only knows slaves and masters. What he dreams of, then, is being master, of issuing orders for others to follow, of inflicting the pain that he has suffered, of exercising power in a vengeance of justification for his life.

Nick Carter thought this as the old man sat passively behind his brothers in the circle. The old man trembled still, his hands between his legs, and the Midwesterner watched him, amused as if the old man were up for sale at a livestock show.

Carter had a plan. Desperate, but a plan nevertheless. When the humiliated old man at last glanced at Carter, Carter stared pointedly at his briefcase across the subterranean room.

''He'll die soon anyway,'' said a third Arab.

''Praise Allah.''

The old man closed his eyes and sang an aching wail that filled the stone room like a chill.

''Shut up!''

One of the Arabs slashed a rifle butt across the old man's chest, sending him somersaulting out of Carter's view. The Midwesterner's amusement grew.

''Don't think we'll ever domesticate these boys,'' he remarked, then laughed. ''Not sure I want to.''

The old man stumbled back into view. He was a stubborn man for a slave. The others ignored the old Arab, settling back to watch the less ordinary spectacle on the rack in the center of their circle. The old man wandered across the room.

"Who else knows about al-Barzani?" the Midwesterner asked Carter.

The wheel moved just enough to make the wires taut.

"Obviously you do," Carter answered with a smile.

The Midwesterner nodded.

The wheel turned.

Needles of pain shot through Carter. His back arched off the ledge. Sweat rushed from his pores.

"*Stop!*"

A shot rang over the heads of the Americans and ricocheted around the stone room. The Arabs and Americans fell flat onto the floor as the bullet whizzed from wall to wall.

TWELVE

For an instant in time, those in the sewer room froze, motionless and shocked.

"What the hell!?" the Midwesterner said sharply, his head turning in confusion, his gun drawn.

"G-Get up!" the old Arab ordered.

The old man in the stained robes held Carter's Luger in both palsied hands. Slowly the old man swung the Luger around the room of Arabs and Americans. Each flinched as the gun shakily faced them.

"G-Get up!" the old man repeated, now worried. The Luger shook harder, dangerously close to firing. Even if the old man's aim was off, a ricocheting bullet was likely to hit someone.

"Put that gun down, dog!" an Arab commanded arrogantly. He scrambled to his feet.

The others followed him up.

"I'll slice your innards and feed them to the godforsaken on the street!" threatened another. He dusted himself off to show his disdain.

The old man's resolve was melting.

"You've got a gun on them," Carter told him. "Order them to drop their weapons and line up against the wall."

The old man glanced at the Luger, then looked up. He stepped forward, revealing Carter's briefcase open on the floor behind him. He swung the Luger around the group.

"Against the wall," the old man said. "Drop your guns."

The Arabs and Americans stared at him but didn't move.

"You can't kill us all at once, imbecile," an Arab with a crooked scar down his cheek said with a sneer.

"You got crabgrass for brains?" the Midwesterner inquired in Arabic.

There were sniggers.

"You're going to have to prove you mean it," Carter said.

"The hospital," the old man wanted to know, "you'll pay?"

"It's the least I can do," Carter said.

The old man nodded, reassured.

"Do it *now*," Carter instructed him.

The old man shot the insulting Arab with the crooked scar through the heart. Blood and tissue splattered the room, and the old man smiled as if he were at a party he'd been planning all his life.

The old man swung the Luger onto the Midwesterner.

"Gooks." The old man smiled wider, imitating the Midwesterner's vicious twang.

"No!" the Midwesterner cried.

The old man shot him through the forehead. The bullet exited out the back of the head, leaving a raw red tunnel as the Midwesterner keeled over onto the bloody floor.

The old man grinned confidently, brandishing the Luger, and the group of Arabs and Americans dropped their arms and backed away from the fallen dead men and against the wall. They raised their hands.

"You!" The old man shook the Luger at another Arab. "You release him!"

The Arab worked on Carter's wires with clammy fingers while the old man happily shouted insults at the others.

". . . and your whores of mothers will curse your jackal fathers for the moment of your birth!" the old man finished, his voice triumphant. The Luger waved.

Carter used his free hand to unwind the wire around his other wrist as the Arab unleashed his ankles and scurried back to the increased safety of the group.

"Are you finished, master?" the old man inquired politely of Carter.

Carter sat on the edge of the ledge. His head whirled.

"Not for at least fifty years," Carter said and grinned.

The old man nodded and danced back to Carter's brief-case, closed it, picked it up—all without taking his cagey eyes off the restless Arabs and Americans—and deposited it beside Carter. He remained in front of Carter, hopping eagerly from foot to foot as his urine dribbled unnoticed onto the floor.

"I would like to go. Yes, I would like to go," the old man said, his eyes alight. "You knew I would. You were so right!"

"Then it's time," Carter said kindly. He gestured at the group against the wall. Their faces were growing dark with impatience. "I'd better—"

"Oh, now," the old man sang. "Oh, my, no. I will take care of them. Yes, yes."

Grinning widely, the old man shot the Arab closest to the door.

"No!" Carter shouted. "There are too many of them!"

The Arab fell flat on his face, and the old man shrugged Carter off. The old man laughed and shot again. He couldn't leave until he had his revenge. He wanted to kill the whole group.

As the Arabs and Americans swelled into an angry juggernaut rolling down on the old man, Carter grabbed the Californian. The Luger flew into the air above the heads of the murderous throng. Carter picked up Wilhel-mina and dragged the struggling Californian out the arch-way door, sadly leaving the old Arab to the price he willingly paid for his vengeance: certain death beneath the fists and feet of his former masters.

The last sounds Carter heard as he pulled the Califor-nian along the stone corridor were the old man's screams.

The Californian's eyes were set too close together. His upper lip protruded over his lower lip. His chin receded into his button-down shirt collar. He had that look of stupid, bulldoglike tenacity that comes from a hard life never understood.

Carter held the Luger on the Californian as the man stood, hands at his sides, in a littered doorway. Beyond them, vegetable and fruit hawkers stared as they pushed carts down the early-morning street. The streets of Baghdad echoed with the calls to prayer from a thousand minarets: "Come to salvation. Prayer is better than sleep . . ."

Carter stood under the lightening sky and wanted to break every bone in the Californian's body. For the old man. Not for his death, but for his miserable life. But the Californian expected that from Carter, and to give him what he expected would not avenge the old man's life.

So Carter patted the Californian down, then took his wallet. *Ralph Desmond, Central Intelligence Agency, Washington, D.C.* The card was official, and not a surprise.

"Cooley bring you?" Carter asked casually, Wilhelmina balanced in his hand.

The Californian looked at Carter. The heavy muscles on his shoulders twitched nervously.

"Don't know," Ralph Desmond replied.

"You were in Vietnam." Carter stared at the snake tattoo on Desmond's arm.

"Off and on," the Californian said, standing straighter.

"The American who was killed, the one from the Midwest, did he bring you here?"

The Californian nodded, gratitude that Carter was not going to kill him dawning in his eyes.

"You talk to any other superiors before you left?" Carter asked.

"No reason to."

Carter sighed.

"Better call in," he advised.

"But Mr. Cooley said . . ."

Carter watched Ralph Desmond, Vietnam veteran, probably well decorated. A hero there. A good guy who somewhere along the line grew unthinking, who settled instead on unquestioned loyalty.

"It's a very dangerous mission," Ralph Desmond said at last. "That's what Mr. Cooley said. He said if we talked about it . . . the Arabs would kill us. He said . . . anyway, it's not our territory to judge these things."

"I see," Carter said. He took out his cigarette case, offered a cigarette to Desmond.

Desmond took it, his fingers trembling slightly. Carter lit the cigarettes.

"How did you know about me?" Carter said. "About AXE? About al-Barzani's operation?"

"Mr. Cooley. Universal Mining and Refining Company has ears all over Washington. That's what Hal said."

Carter smoked.

"Hal the dead guy?" Carter asked.

Desmond nodded and looked at his cigarette.

"We've been together since 'Nam."

"Where does Cooley stay?"

"Don't know." Desmond dragged on the cigarette. "Hal said there was a big party tonight, though. Said Cooley and all of them would be there."

"Where?"

Desmond gave him directions to the eastern outskirts of Baghdad. They smoked. Desmond studied the gold-embossed monograms on Carter's cigarettes but said nothing. When Desmond finished, he walked down the busy street toward a telephone booth.

Carter watched only a moment before he turned to walk in the opposite direction, thinking about Khartoum and his assignment in the Sudan. He found an old hotel with freshly washed steps and went in. The Egyptian on the White Nile would have to wait. A big party with Cooley and al-Barzani could be a celebration . . . and an opportunity to find out what al-Barzani's organization planned. It could be a quicker answer than the uncertainty that awaited with a half-dead Egyptian in a village far away.

Carter got a key from the hotel's desk clerk and ordered

a meal sent to his room. He went upstairs, locked his door, pulled down the shade, and took off all his clothes. He went into the bathroom. First he would take care of his wounds and shower, then he'd eat and sleep through the day. He would be ready for tonight. . . .

THIRTEEN

At twilight, Baghdad is a city of mystery. Centuries ago it was a leading trade center in Mesopotamia, built on the Tigris River in three concentric circles by a caliph with vision. The innermost wall enclosed the palace of the caliph and his successors. The second wall contained the army quarters. The third wall enclosed the homes of the people. Outside the city walls were the merchants' quarters and bazaars.

Now the walls have mostly disappeared, and the city has homogenized into wealth and poverty. Busy bazaars and heavy modern construction. Free-flowing streams of people in colorful robes intent on carrying their pasts into the Western present.

As Carter rode in the taxi toward the city's suburbs, he watched the people begin work and end it, greet their families, pat their dogs, and do all the ordinary little actions that make them people. He sat in the taxi in the formal evening clothes he had rented late that afternoon, his briefcase on the floor, and stared at the centuries-old buildings mixed with the new, at the gold-domed mosques, at the Cadillacs. Across the rooftops from the highest minarets pealed the calls to evening prayer, and Nick Carter felt Baghdad's storybook magnificence from the back seat of a Chevrolet taxi. It was a mystery, this city in twilight, shading out the differences between the old and the new until only the mystery was important.

Carter's destination turned out to be a palace behind a

tall whitewashed stucco wall. ''This is where General al-Gaillani lives,'' the taxi driver commented in Kurdish. ''I took him and his wife to the airport this morning. Wonder who's giving the party?'' Carter had the driver pass the palace slowly and then stop a block away.

Carter got out, paid him, and strolled slowly back along the street. General al-Gaillani was one of the four highest-ranking generals in Iraq, far superior to al-Barzani.

Limousines carrying people in evening dress passed through the heavy wrought-iron gates where two guards checked invitations. The guards were on the right, operating from a tile-roofed kiosk. Beyond them Carter could see the palace arise in a long rectangle with sloping blue-tiled roofs and towers at each corner. An electrified fence topped the whitewashed stucco outer wall and ran across the palace's roof. Guards, gates, and fences give a false sense of security to even the most fearful.

The limousines had backed up to the street. Carter in his black tuxedo squatted to the left of a limousine as it sedately drove up the long driveway past a flat reflecting pool in which lilies and swans were illuminated by underwater lights. A thick odor of exotic flowers filled the air. The guards at the kiosk on the right were already checking the next limousine's invitation.

Carter's immediate danger was over.

He strode confidently past the protection of his limousine and up to the pillared entry. He handed his white silk scarf to the immaculately robed butler at the door but kept his briefcase, then walked into the music and laughter of the party.

Another butler handed him a glass of champagne from a silver tray. A woman in robes threaded with gold took his arm and escorted him to a table laden with food. Proper clothes and good manners make even the uninvited guest desirable.

Carter scanned the room above the woman's head. There was no sign of Cooley or al-Barzani or even Elena and her lieutenant.

''I don't see General al-Gaillani,'' Carter said casually

in Arabic. "Too bad he has to miss his own party."

"Ah, yes," the woman said softly in the tones of the well-bred. She ate a shrimp. "It could not be helped." A diamond bracelet sparkled on her arm. "They would have been here, but Farah's mother took ill. They would be better in the safety of the palace."

"Safety?" Carter picked up a long silver stick on which fruits had been alternated with tomatoes and olives.

The woman had doe eyes, deeply set in smooth olive skin surrounded by veiling. She was not Elena Markova. Not even tinted contact lenses could change Elena's blue eyes into the black ones with long dark lashes now appraising Carter.

"Yes, of course. Why we are here. The . . ." She stopped. "Who are you?"

Carter clicked his heels together and bowed.

"Pardon me," he said suavely. "I'm Michael McKinney, an associate of Mr. Cooley's from the United States." He took her perfectly manicured hand and kissed it.

She looked at him calmly.

"And you?" he said.

"Princess Jessem." She ate another shrimp and watched him. "I'm a friend of Farah al-Gaillani. She asked me to take care of her guests. But I'm not doing a very good job, am I? You'll be all right now. I must see to the others."

She moved away in a swirl of gold and musky perfume. She paused to talk to a couple, he in an Iraqi colonel's uniform and the woman in orange silk, then she went to the butler at the door. The couple stared at Carter, and then the butler did.

Carter moved away through the crowded two-story-high room, sipping his champagne, toward the back. The crowd had grown since his arrival, with almost half the men in high-ranking officers' uniforms. Carter found a hallway. The butler was now moving through the party room too, his eyes glancing from side to side.

Carter walked briskly down the winding hall, around corners, pausing at doors and listening. At last he found one where voices in animated conversation rumbled. He listened, could hear only occasional words, but the voices of Colonel al-Barzani and Melvin Cooley belonged to two of the speakers. The third voice he didn't recognize.

"Now!" al-Barzani said.

". . . soldiers outside," the third said.

"Where do . . . go?" Cooley asked.

The voices were growing distant, almost as if the men were moving to the other side of the room. Carter heard a door open and bang closed.

Carter raced down the hall looking for a back exit.

Shots rang outside.

Shots thundered in the palace.

Carter found French doors opening onto a back garden. Two shapes disappeared down the bricked walk. Soldiers with poised rifles closed in protectively behind the shapes and blocked off the sidewalk.

Carter returned at a dead run down the hall back into the immense room of the party where more soldiers with the patches of al-Barzani's Zab Brigade on their shoulders were pouring in through windows and doors.

Generals and colonels lay dead on the marble floor.

Women and servants screamed.

Smoke curled in the air above as the soldiers shot into the mass of wealth and power. Surveying the scene from a balcony, al-Barzani stood with his arms crossed over his chest. He smiled at the success of his beginning coup.

Carter turned at the sound of unified shouts. The butler pointed a rifle at Carter and waved his arm at the soldiers.

Carter ducked.

And ran straight through the center of the throng.

Smashing ribs and jaws.

Through a window, around a corner, and to the limousines parked beside the reflecting pool. He fell into the front seat of the first one, shoved Wilhelmina into the driver's face, and ordered him out of there.

FOURTEEN

Tanks and armored cars rumbled through Baghdad's night. Arabs stood on corners and watched them, puzzled, then with dawning realization dashed back into doorways and shadows. Occasional gunfire sounded in bursts as Carter and the driver entered the heart of Baghdad. Carter ordered the driver to stop at the hotel with the freshly washed steps.

Carter bounded up the stairs and to his room, ripping off his tie and cummerbund as he ran. Once inside, he locked the door and picked up the telephone.

Hawk must have been waiting for his call. He was put directly through.

"Riyadh, too," Carter mused. "I thought as much."

Hawk's voice was tired and worried as he continued. "We don't know much. Cecil Young's report wasn't complete. All hell was breaking loose there, too. That demented fanatic Mujahid is trying to seize power. The prime minister is dead. The king has vanished. MI5 doesn't know what's happened to Young. The connection went dead in the middle of his report."

Carter pressed the receiver into his ear.

"I'm sorry about Young," he said.

"Yes. Very capable man. Too damned bad," Hawk said gruffly. "Was Cooley at the party?"

"Earlier, before the shooting started. And some of the soldiers wearing the Zab Brigade patch were Americans, I think. Westerners, anyway. I didn't stop to chat."

Hawk was silent. Carter knew he was puffing on his cigar.

"I'll take care of the Americans from this end," Hawk said. "That damned fool Cooley and his international corporation! You get onto al-Barzani. I want some answers!"

Carter dressed again in the all-black jumpsuit, abandoning the tuxedo in the hotel room. Carrying his briefcase, he walked out into the ominous quiet of the city. The streets were deserted now except for an occasional stray dog or cat wandering among garbage or stopping to urinate beside the scraggly trees that dotted the sidewalks.

Carter walked in shadows as he made his way along the street. In the distance he heard a truck with a loudspeaker blaring as it moved slowly down the silent streets.

"All is well! Keep calm and stay in your homes! We will take care of you! Keep calm! All is well!"

Carter walked toward the sound, stopping under the shadowed arch of an ancient building. He picked up a rock.

The truck rumbled toward his block. There would be soldiers around the truck, guarding it.

He waited, thought about a cigarette, hefted the rock in his hand.

The truck's lights made beams down the center of the street, beams that moved with the silhouettes of the soldiers in front.

First came six soldiers spread across the width of the street. They marched tall and straight, proud in the security of their cause and the success of their coup.

Then came the truck, a Ford F-500, painted in camouflage colors, with the loudspeaker mounted over the cab.

Last came six more soldiers, stepping smartly.

Carter threw the rock hard against a wall three buildings back.

The corporal barked an order.

Two soldiers from the rear peeled off and ran back toward the sound.

The truck and the other soldiers continued.

Carter waited, his stiletto in his palm.

Eventually the two soldiers came back up the street to return to their guard duties. They were shaking their heads and muttering at the bad nerves of their corporal.

Carter threw Hugo, a speeding sliver of light, into the heart of the more distant soldier. Carter didn't want to ruin the other's uniform. The other soldier looked to be the right size.

As the first soldier fell, the other automatically squatted, stared around the street, and whispered urgently to his fallen comrade. When there was no response from his friend and no other sign of danger in the street, the soldier crab walked to the body and leaned over it.

Carter dashed silently from his shadow.

Yanked back the head of the soldier.

Snapped the neck in a single smooth motion that left the man brain dead.

Carter dragged the twitching body back into the shadow beneath the arch.

FIFTEEN

Baghdad seemed to be holding its breath. Windows were dark. There was no rioting or looting. Shooting had stopped. The only movements were of animals and furtive humans hiding from shadow to shadow with nowhere else to go. Far off, loudspeakers blared, the only breathing in a city gone into shock.

Carter adjusted the Zab Brigade uniform. It was tight in the shoulders and loose in the waist, but he didn't care. It would serve its purpose adequately. He picked up his briefcase and the fallen soldier's rifle and marched down the sidewalk under the starry sky. Occasionally a curtain would move and he knew someone there had enough curiosity to overcome good sense or fear.

As he approached al-Barzani's headquarters, activity picked up. A tank sat outside the door. A soldier handed up a sheaf of written orders, and the tank groaned into movement down the street. Armored cars and troop-carrying trucks were parked along the cordoned-off street.

A platoon of soldiers with backpacks and rifles were being loaded into one of the Ford trucks. A sergeant walked from driver to driver, handing out more orders.

Carter strode like any soldier into the well-lit headquarters. He heard a teletype in a back room. Well-modulated voices made reports in an adjoining room with a map of the Middle East laid out on a banquet-sized table. Telephones rang. Western and Arabic soldiers with the Zab Brigade patch walked purposefully up and down the hall

90

and into rooms carrying reports or supplies. As meetings formed and reformed, some of the offices were left empty.

The headquarters had no sense of frenzy, only well-ordered planning. It was a smoothly running machine.

There was no sign of al-Barzani.

But Elena and her lieutenant were standing in the doorway of his upstairs office.

From the end of the hall, Carter watched them talk. At last the lieutenant swept Elena into a deep kiss, then pushed her off, patting her fanny as he sent her down the hall.

Elena walked away with purpose, as if on assignment, perhaps for the lieutenant and the al-Barzani organization.

Carter strode down the steps well ahead of her. He ducked into an office that had been vacant before he had gone upstairs.

The rifle was against his neck.

A cold muzzle that bore sharply into his flesh.

And the door closed. Carter's shoulders moved a fraction of an inch as he readied his own rifle.

"Don't!" the voice warned Carter in Arabic. "Even a twitch and I'll kill you!"

Carter knew the voice. One of the Arabs from the sewer.

"Wouldn't dream of it," Carter said in Arabic.

There was a grunt.

The rifle was gone.

Carter turned.

Ralph Desmond, the Californian from the CIA, stood over the dead Arab and grinned at Carter. He held a switchblade dripping blood.

"I made that call," Desmond said.

The Arab's throat was slit neatly in an arc from ear to ear. Blood poured onto the floor. The head angled unnaturally to the side.

"Was the information useful?" Carter asked.

"Straightened me out," Desmond said. "Thanks."

Carter clapped him on the shoulder, then looked again at the dead Arab.

"This'll spoil your cover," Carter said. "Better tell them I did it."

Desmond grinned wider and nodded.

Carter slipped out the door and down the hall toward the front steps where he could see Elena's curvy back. She had on navy trousers, a lightweight sweater, and sneakers. She tapped her foot impatiently.

Carter found another empty office, picked up a sheaf of papers from the desk, and returned to the hall to join the organized bedlam as cover for watching Elena.

At last a green Fiat drove up. The soldier behind the wheel hopped out, tipped his cap, and Elena got in.

Carter marched down the street after the disappearing Fiat.

Hot-wiring a car is not a requirement to be a Killmaster. Neither is swimming well, using the right fork, speaking a dozen languages and as many dialects, knowing how to drive all sorts of vehicles, adding a column of four-digit figures in your head, or any other number of seemingly disparate skills. But flexibility *is* a requirement, and flexibility demands unpredicted skills.

Carter found an old Toyota parked at a deserted curb in the next block. He started it, got in, and drove off after Elena. She had a purpose about her that she wasn't trying to hide. She was so definite, so certain, that Carter had chosen to follow her rather than stay looking for al-Barzani. She had a plan, and she had information. Carter had a better chance with her.

Carter was able to catch up with her because of the emptiness of the streets. All he had to do was turn off the Toyota's motor to listen for hers. She wasn't heading in the direction of her apartment.

Eventually other cars joined them on the streets, and he had to swing onto the same block with her so he wouldn't lose her. The cars were all heading in the same direction.

Baghdad's airport. Escape.

Mechanics moved around the small jet, filling it and checking instruments. Airport guards and Zab Brigade soldiers patrolled around the jet and the other small private jets lined up on the tarmac.

Elena Markova stood beside the jet, her arms full of papers. She was talking to a tall, beefy man with a Slavic face and dead eyes. He had the paleness of northern Russia and the stiff bearing of a Communist official. Elena and the Russian talked quietly, agreeing on decisions.

Carter held his rifle in both hands. If he kept it, he might be ordered on guard duty in the airport. It was much better to have only the briefcase. That way he appeared to be a courier.

Carter threw the rifle into a drainpipe and walked around the jet, out of sight of Elena, and down the line of small private jets, looking for what he needed.

The airport was in turmoil, lines at ticket counters extending thirty and forty yards. Zab Brigade soldiers, airport security guards, and regular Iraqi soldiers milled through the terminal and out onto the tarmac. There was no fighting between the Zab Brigade soldiers and the regular Iraqi soldiers. It was almost as if there were a truce between the two factions of the coup while they waited for something special to happen or be decided.

Carter crossed the terminal and moved onto the tarmac he'd driven past earlier while following Elena. The two MIG-23s he remembered were still there, now fueled, with two Zab Brigade soldiers and two regular Iraqi soldiers guarding them.

The two sleek jets glistened in the light of the rising moon, their long needle noses pointed north. They were Flogger-Es in the MIG-23 series, the export version of Russia's primary air-to-air tactical aircraft, the Flogger-B. The Flogger-E is equipped to a lower standard than the Soviet Air Force's Flogger-Bs. They have a smaller radar range, a shorter nose radome, no undernose laser range-finder, and no Doppler navigation equipment. Besides Iraq, Russia has equipped Algeria, Cuba, and Libya with the lower-standard Flogger-Es, but no one complains. Their killing capability is good; they're armed with Atoll missiles and a GSh-23 gun. And Russia doesn't worry. The pilots being equal, the Flogger-Es were less defensi-

ble and therefore would always come out second to the
Flogger-Bs.

Carter walked up to one of the regular Iraqi soldiers
guarding the MIG-23s.

"You must turn over your rifles to me," Carter announced in Arabic. "The People of Purity will take over
here now."

The soldier stared at Carter.

"I need to see orders," the soldier said.

"What's wrong?" shouted one of the Brigade soldiers
to Carter. He walked toward Carter at a fast clip.

"Changeover to the Brigade," Carter said and opened
the briefcase.

Carter fished through the papers, looking for the
nonexistent orders, and all four soldiers gathered around.
Waiting for orders was part of the profession.

They watched the briefcase.

Carter kicked the closest one in the belly and sent him
spinning back, vomiting.

Carter jabbed his elbow in the most distant one's teeth,
felt the burns of tooth cuts in his arm as the Iraqi screamed,
spitting teeth and blood.

Carter locked his arms around the necks of the middle
two and crashed their heads together, knocking them
unconscious.

Nick Carter, Killmaster, did all this in thirty seconds.
Then he ran over to the two who weren't out and chopped
them lightly on the back of the neck. He needed time, and
this quartet wouldn't be up for quite a while.

He climbed into the single-seat variable-geometry
fighter jet. He found the pilot's parachute and backpack. It
is wise to be prepared. He put the Luger and some of his
tools from the briefcase into the backpack, then put on his
jumpsuit, the pilot's parachute, backpack, and head-
phones.

By the time he'd warmed up the jet and taxied onto the
runway leading to Elena's jet, she was gone.

Her jet was at the end of a distant runway, ready for
takeoff.

As Carter rolled his jet closer to hers, a controller's quiet questioning from the tower of who Carter was and what-in-hell-did-he-think-he-was-doing changed into screams of anger and frustration.

Elena had clearance. What had been her lie to get that?

A good two miles behind, Carter followed her down the runway and into the dawn air where the moon hung in superfluous splendor in the rose-streaked sky.

They flew west toward the Mediterranean coast, toward Tripoli, Beirut, Sidon, and Tyre.

Phillips's claws dug into the half-dead Egyptian's shoulders. Phillips shook the limp body, rattled it until the teeth chattered and Phillips's arms at last grew numb.

"Shit."

Phillips glanced at the native nurse huddled in a ball in the corner of the white hospital room. She'd tried to leave three times. She whimpered quietly, a bruise darkening on her left cheek. Her left eye was swollen shut. She was like a trapped animal. Any moment he expected her to bolt again.

Phillips glared at the unconscious Egyptian. The Egyptian might as well be dead. Totally useless, and no sign of change.

Phillips spat on the floor. He marched across the room to a cabinet. Locked. Phillips took out a Python revolver, ran his thumb over the handle and up over the barrel.

The girl squealed and ducked.

He barked a short laugh and shot the combination lock off the cabinet. Inside was what he wanted. He didn't know what it was exactly, but he knew it was there.

He found a syringe and stared along the rows of small bottles, samples from pharmaceutical companies. He looked at the strange words. Finally he picked a bottle containing an amber liquid. He took it and the syringe to the girl.

He filled the syringe in front of her wide, frightened eyes.

"No! Please!" she begged in dialect.

"You or the Egyptian," Phillips said.

He wanted to bury his face in her hair, take deep breaths of the natural perfume of wild flowers and woodsmoke.

Instead, he grabbed a fistful of the black hair and yanked her head back. He held the syringe up.

"Your choice," he said. "I only want to talk to the Egyptian. I don't want to kill either of you."

"Me, then," the girl said simply and closed her eyes.

"Bah!"

Phillips threw her under the Egyptian's hospital bed. She rolled into a fetal position, a baby with a whim of iron. He couldn't break her. But he could kill her. Only . . . he didn't want to.

Phillips stood over the Egyptian, furious and helpless.

He was a boy again, running down the red brick street in Montreal, that bastard Monsieur Robaire after him, waving a butcher knife. His mother had married Monsieur Robaire for food and shelter. Phillips had been four years old. By the time he was six, he'd run away from home for the first time. Monsieur Robaire caught him and dragged him back.

"You run again, kid," his mother's husband had said, "and I'll cut those little balls off." He'd sliced the air twice with the butcher knife, inches from Phillips's nose. Phillips had believed him.

Still, he ran away again and again, until at nine he'd hidden so well his stepfather couldn't find him. Three years later a social worker discovered Phillips living with the rats in a different section of Montreal. To convince him to go into a halfway house, the social worker had explained that Monsieur Robaire had married Phillips's mother because he liked little boys. "Child sexual abuse and brutality," the social worker's report had said.

The social worker's investigation was designed to make Phillips feel better so he'd want to stay in the halfway house. Phillips didn't care. He didn't particularly even remember the abuse the social worker had documented. What Phillips did remember was running down that damned brick street between the florists and bakeries, smelling the scents of fresh food and fresh-cut flowers, seeing the clean, rich people go into the shops and knowing that with no money and that bastard Monsieur Robaire chasing him he'd never be able to stop and have them.

It was a funny memory, Phillips knew, and it was the only one he hadn't been able to get rid of. He hadn't entered the halfway house. The social worker had been a do-gooding idiot. She wouldn't leave him alone. He'd had to kill her.

Now he stared down at the Egyptian and wanted only one thing—to kill him, too. But he couldn't, not and make more money from Hawk and Blenkochev and maybe even some other governments he hadn't had time to consider.

He crossed his arms. If the Egyptian would only move, he'd feel some hope.

Then he heard the jets again.

"Stay here!" he commanded the girl under the bed.

She didn't move, and he walked outside into the clearing. The morning sky was bright and clear. It would be another hot day in the village.

Unmarked jets swooped above the White Nile and the village. Eight of them. He heard the engines of slower aircraft as the jets darted back and forth through the blue sky.

The slower planes flew lower. They were transports. He held his arms tight over his thin chest as he continued to watch.

Parachutists dropped like tiny white marshmallows in a ragged line from the transports. He grinned and cocked his head. Then he heard the land vehicles and power launches.

SIXTEEN

Nick Carter maneuvered his jet from cloud to cloud as he followed Elena Markova west toward Beirut, Carter's original assignment. Beirut, where the civil strife of Lebanon was a bloody symbol of Arab disunity, could be Elena's destination, but her jet angled south, away from Lebanon, and skirted Israel and the Sinai. Flying a Soviet-made jet, Carter had no desire to enter Israeli airspace. One thing the United States had done for their Israeli allies was train first-class fighter pilots. And as good as Carter was, he was flying an inferior jet made in an enemy country. The Israelis would fire first, ask questions later. That's how they had survived.

The clouds thinned out, and Carter dropped behind, following Elena on the jet's radar. She would be able to spot him, too, so he continued to fly diversionary directions, always keeping her on his radar screen. To her, he would be just another blip.

Carter followed Elena over the shimmering Red Sea. North he could barely see the slash in the earth called the Suez Canal or, as Moshe Dayan had said, the world's greatest antitank ditch.

They were entering Egypt where, if Hawk's information was correct, someone had known something about the Shiites' plans.

Carter considered whether Elena would land in Cairo.

Post-Sadat Egypt was slowly reentering Middle Eastern politics and regaining acceptance. But the Egyptians wanted no more conflict, and the Shiites would find few sympathizers there.

Elena Markova could continue west to Libya where the erratic dictator Colonel Muammar Kaddafi preached worldwide revolution, opposed peace talks with Israel, and threatened to cut off Libyan oil to the United States. The charismatic Kaddafi was revered by many in the Arab world, particularly for his strong religious stands. He'd even formed a separate Libyan army called the Islamic Legion to fight for Islamic causes. In 1983 he had sent two thousand Libyan regular troops and three thousand Islamic Legion fighters into Chad to help the rebels led by former Chadian President Goukouni Wedeye return the government to stronger religious footing—and to bring it in closer political alignment with Libya.

Libya was a definite possibility.

Kaddafi was just the sort of leader al-Barzani and Prince Mujahid would admire.

But the jet turned south.

And now Carter knew where she was going.

The Sudan.

She would have to stop briefly to refuel, but with his extra tanks, Carter would easily make the flight.

"Nicky-babe." Elena Markova's voice was suddenly in his earphones. "I know it's you. Go screw yourself."

"Elena!"

She cut off transmission, and her jet blipped off his radar screen. She had spotted him at last and put on a burst of speed.

Carter pushed the throttle. He'd had a good run behind her. The Tumansky R-29B turbojet engine shot the jet forward. Since Elena knew about him, there was no longer any need to stay hidden. Her jet was private, unarmed. She couldn't fight him, so she would try to lose him. But she wouldn't have the speed of his fighter. If he was right about her destination, he would have plenty of time to find her there.

Carter flew south, eventually over the remarkable Aswan Dam and Lake Nasser—built by Russian technol-

ogy learned from the United States—and followed the
Nile River south into the Sudan and the radiating Nubian
Desert. Occasional commercial jets and flocks of jet
fighters came on his screen. He was careful to maintain
speed and keep a low profile.

He flew a straight line, the air clear and glassy beneath
the brilliant sun, the ground disappearing now in a mass of
patchworked colors.

Near Khartoum, the Nile River splits into its two major
tributaries, the White Nile and the Blue Nile. Khartoum
means "elephant trunk," referring to the narrow strip of
land at the juncture of the two rivers. He followed the
White Nile south through farmland, forest, and jungle into
the southern Sudan.

There he found her.

Elena's jet was skimming over the treetops beside the
White Nile as if she were looking for something. He
admired the steadiness of her control. He smiled and
remembered her passion in bed. Then he leaned forward,
seizing the jet's controls like a vise.

She was being shot at.

From the ground.

Elena's jet swerved, evading.

Too late.

It was a land-to-air missile that got her.

A flash of fire and a gray puff of smoke.

She was close enough to the ground that her crippled jet
never had a chance to spiral. It did a nose dive, slid into the
trees, and disappeared.

A bonfire shot up above the forest. Carter circled
above. Elena Markova's jet would be nothing but cinders.
And Elena. . . .

Carter's throat was tight. He circled lower, then shot
straight up, the jet's cantilevered wings slicing air. He
leveled out at twenty thousand feet, rocking the wings
from side to side as he soared into Equatoria and then back
north to the White Nile. Once again over the fire-spitting
trees, he grimly rocked his wings, a tribute and farewell to
Elena Markova.

A missile shot by his left side.

He ducked automatically, veering off to the right.

He brought the jet low, too low for another missile.

Suddenly there were two jets on his tail.

Flogger-Es, like his own.

Troops were below him in a clearing.

The Flogger-Es shot red-streaking bullets at him, peppering his wings.

He veered again, then flew up. The Flogger-Es pursued, and he pushed the jet to tolerance, flipping between the enemy jets, shooting into the cockpit of one.

He had a glimpse of a startled then angry face through the shattered glass. The enemy jet went into a fast spiral.

Carter didn't have time to watch where it crashed.

The other Flogger-E was behind him again.

He dipped low, swooping above the troops. Some of them raised their rifles and shot at him. They were too far away to have range.

The remaining Flogger-E followed him.

Carter shot his jet upward again, but this time the other pilot was quick. He came right up after Carter.

Carter flipped over, veered left, and circled upright.

He had the enemy jet in front of him. Carter shot into the jet's tail section.

The enemy jet burst into flames. The pilot pushed open the cockpit and ejected. His parachute unfolded, and he drifted toward the ground.

Smoke was billowing from Carter's jet. He'd been hit but hadn't noticed.

The jet was sluggish.

Losing power fast.

Carter looked down and saw the clearing where the soldiers had shot at him. He tried the controls again. He wouldn't be able to land the jet. He set the automatic pilot, aimed the jet into the uninhabited jungle, opened the cockpit, and bailed out.

He was dizzy from the sudden feeling of free fall.

He jerked straight as the parachute popped open and caught air. He tugged on the shrouds, maneuvering south of the clearing. About a mile south.

It is dangerous for a parachutist to land in trees. The

branches will catch the chute and leave the jumper dangling fifteen feet above the ground. The jumper has to cut himself free and risks breaking a leg or his back in the fall. Or, worse, as he's coming in, a sharp branch can impale the jumper, leaving him wounded or dead.

Carter tugged on the parachute shrouds, urgently searching for a clearing in the forest of acacia, ebony, and mahogany. He didn't want to expose himself by landing on the riverbank.

He was getting lower.

He had to make a decision.

The riverbank was ahead, inviting, overgrown with flowers and low bushes.

To the left across the sea of treetops he suddenly saw what looked like a tunnel—almost a well—deep and dark down through the towering trees. Probably not more than a dozen feet wide.

He angled toward it.

His feet touched the tops of the trees, He was a dead weight on the end of a winch. His legs slid down in the branches beside the clearing. He was sweating.

The branches caught at his jumpsuit and backpack. He kicked away, watching the shrouds and the deflating parachute above. The parachute mustn't sink into the trees. There it would become entangled.

He was so low that his feet touched a heavy branch.

His trained instincts responded.

He jumped off the branch.

Into the center of the tunnel.

Came down fast and clear.

And rolled into the fall.

He jumped to his feet. He was safe, sweating like a glass of Jack Daniel's, but safe.

Carter gathered the parachute and shrouds, packed them together, and kicked the duff from the base of a mahogany tree. In the distance, an elephant trumpeted. Another answered. Carter put the bundle under the tree and kicked the duff back to cover it.

He took Wilhelmina out of the backpack and checked

the pilot's supplies. He found what he needed: a compass. In the denseness of the forest, all directions were the same.

Carter walked north.

Thin rays of sunlight filtered through the leafy branches, splashing onto grass, leaves, flowers, and moss. The thick smell of vegetation filled the air. Birds called and monkeys chattered.

He occasionally glimpsed shy animals and birds before they ducked into hiding. He watched the sky whenever there was an opening in the canopy of branches and leaves above. Then he would see the gray smoke, probably from Elena Markova's jet. He would sigh, trudging on, mourning in his own way the passing of an enemy who because of the similarity of her way of living was intimately close to him.

He was approaching the clearing. His instincts told him that it lay about five hundred feet ahead.

He stopped when he realized that the only sounds he heard were his own quiet feet on the forest floor.

He listened.

Not even a twig snapped.

There was a hush in the forested jungle, an unnatural hush that signaled shock.

Carter crept forward.

Brushed aside rubber and papyrus plants.

Stared into the clearing.

At the remains of a devastated village.

SEVENTEEN

The bloody, broken bodies of natives lay strewn about the clearing. Dead dogs still kept guard at the doorways of the crushed, smoldering thatched huts. Shreds of door cloths waved limply in the hot air. White, horned cattle with pink noses lay dead, gutted by gunfire, still tethered to their stakes. Carter wiped his sleeve across his burning eyes. The air stank of smoke, burned flesh, and death.

This was why the soldiers had been in the clearing, with jets nearby to protect them.

The soldiers had been destroying the village.

Carter had a hunch why.

He noted the tracks of trucks and jeeps in the clearing's dust, and saw that they headed west.

Then he looked across the clearing to the remains of a large building built of boards. The interior had been white and now shone darkly in the shadows of overhanging trees where it lay collapsed.

Carter had a choice. He could stay within the wall of jungle that outlined the clearing, risking noise and slow progress, or he could move onto the hard-packed dusty perimeter that marked the line beyond which the natives would not let the relentless tentacles of the jungle reach.

Carter stepped onto the dirt compacted by feet and hooves, readjusted his backpack, and felt the friendly security of Wilhelmina in his hand.

The building across the clearing must be the native hospital that Hawk had told him about. And inside could

104

still be Major General Farouk of the Egyptian secret police.

Major General Farouk would be the reason the soldiers had come—either to save him or kill him. They had left no natives alive to report which. It had been a massacre, and there were no soldiers' bodies in the compound.

Carter walked around the perimeter of the flattened village, passing baskets and crude toys, recently washed undergarments hanging on a baobob tree to dry, a dead little girl ripped apart by a machine gun, millet in a gourd to be ground by a wooden pestle nearby, more dead bodies.

He heard the moans from what must have been the front porch of the hospital.

They were soft moans, without hope.

He pulled off boards and crude shingles from the collapsed roof that covered the pile where the sounds came from.

"Hold on," he said in Dinka dialect.

He saw the white skirt first, then brown naked legs pulled up tight against the white bodice where the young breasts heaved for air.

"You'll be all right," Carter reassured her. He stroked the nurse's hair from her forehead.

She had been hit across the head, a bloody welt showing big enough to knock a man twice her weight unconscious. Beneath that were older bruises on her eye and cheek.

"Stay here," Carter told her. "Don't move."

She started to nod, then thought better of it.

"Thank you," she murmured and opened her eyes.

She screamed.

She stared at Nick Carter and screamed again and again, her knees under her chin, and Carter saw the ripped underpants above the triangle of dark hair, and the blood and other fluids dried on her legs. The bruises that showed struggle. She'd been raped.

Carter dropped the pack from his back and started going through it as she screamed.

"I won't hurt you," he said calmly.

He took out a lightweight square of cloth from the pilot's survival gear and unfolded it into a blanket. He covered her.

Her screams were hoarse now, her lips dry and cracked.

"Who did this?" Carter asked, looking for a mild tranquilizer.

The sudden weight on his back knocked him over and left him gasping for air.

He rolled onto his feet, Wilhelmina in one hand, as he swung the other up.

"Nya, no!" the girl cried.

Carter stopped.

And watched.

The young male Nilote held a heavy club high over his head. He wore only a loincloth and beads, and he had two bullet holes caked with mud and blood on his chest. His fierce eyes glazed, then cleared. He swayed, dizzy.

Carter grabbed the young man's shoulders. The Dinka swung the club limply. Carter ducked and let the man's weight carry him forward into Carter's arms. Carter laid him on the ground.

The nurse was struggling to her feet.

"Stay down," Carter ordered. "You'll be sick."

"*White men!*" the girl spat and crawled toward the young man.

Carter took her arm to help her. She bit him.

"Your choice, ma'am."

She leaned over the young man, crooning, and covered him with the pilot's blanket.

Carter found a packet of sulfa and bandages.

She took them from him without looking and tended the unconscious man's wounds.

"Aspirin," she said at last.

"Aspirin?"

"Nothing stronger," she said. She glanced over the compound at the bloody bodies swarming with flies. "I have work to do."

He found aspirin in the pilot's pack. She took them and

sat on her heels. She closed her eyes. Tears spread down her cheeks.

"Where's the Egyptian?" Carter asked.

She wiped an arm across her face, stood up, and walked to the body of an old woman collapsed beside a dung cooking fire. The old woman had white cottony hair, the round self-inflicted scars that Dinkas admire as marks of beauty, and pain on her dead face.

"The Egyptian is inside," the nurse said, waving a hand in the direction of the hospital's debris. "But you are too late. He is dead." She leaned over the old woman and pushed flies away.

Carter picked his way over the collapsed hospital building, over splintered boards, broken pottery, crushed chairs. There was a mound. He saw the metal foot of a hospital bed. He cleared away boards and shingles. The Egyptian was pale with death. Machine gun bullets had cut him like a chain saw from chin to testicles. Flies swarmed greedily.

Carter shook his head and mopped his face. He surveyed the wreckage of what had been the hospital.

"Where's the Egyptian's note?" he shouted at the nurse.

She shook her head and shrugged. She had moved to a cluster of bodies. Parents and four or five children. She sobbed.

Carter kicked at the boards and shingles, trying to find the floor.

"Did the doctor have a bag of medicines?" Carter asked.

"In the cabinet."

Carter found a gray metal cabinet pitched over onto its doors. He cleaned off the debris and stood the cabinet upright. Inside the base was an old leather doctor's bag.

He took it to the nurse.

She had moved again, making her way from body to body, crying and examining each.

"They're all dead," she sobbed.

He followed her around the compound, carrying the bag for her, as she looked for life.

At last she returned to the young man who was still unconscious under the pilot's blanket. She sat beside him.

"Only us," she said and took the young man's hand. She looked shyly at Carter. There was gratitude on her tear-streaked face. "This is Nya. I'm Anya."

"Nick Carter, ma'am." He squatted in front of her. "I'd like to know what happened."

"Will you find them?" she wanted to know. Her eyes blazed. "Kill them?"

"First I have to know what happened."

"They . . . they wanted *him*." She looked at the hospital and back at Carter. The tears had made shiny streaks down her dust-covered face. Wood splinters clung to her disheveled black hair. She had soft, even features, a pretty girl made into a courageous harridan by circumstances.

"The soldiers?"

"Many soldiers," she said. "We couldn't stop them. They had guns. The Egyptian didn't wake up, so they killed him. And . . . they killed us."

"I see." Carter nodded. "And you?"

Tears again coursed down her cheeks, but she held her head high.

"Phillips," was all she said.

Carter understood. While the soldiers had been busy killing the villagers, Phillips had raped her. Ironically, he had probably saved her life.

Carter watched her.

"Do you have somewhere to go?" he asked gently.

"We will go to the next village. Upstream. I will take the doctor's medicines with me. Nya's wounds are high. Not in the heart or arteries. I will take the bullets out there."

Carter stood up.

"I wish I could help you more," he said.

Carter picked up the young man and carried him to the riverbank. The nurse followed with the bag. Carter put the wounded man in a canoe. She got in and Carter set the bag at her feet.

"Thank you," she said and looked up. "I would very much like you to kill those soldiers. All of them."

Carter smiled. "I'll do what I can."

She nodded, picked up a paddle, and Carter pushed the canoe into the White Nile. She struggled a moment against the current, then pointed the canoe upstream. She paddled steadily, a valiant figure in white.

Carter returned to the compound and the sound of buzzing flies. Beyond them the jungle was returning to normalcy. Parrots shrieked and monkeys chattered.

Carter looked at the truck and jeep tracks heading west. Who were the soldiers? What were they doing in such large numbers in a remote jungle? Why had they destroyed an innocent and unimportant village? And was the Egyptian the only reason?

Carter noted the footprints made by heavy boots mixed among the naked footprints of the villagers. They were well-equipped troops, with everything from land-to-air missiles to jets. Had the renegade Islamic coups reached even into this jungle?

Carter picked up Wilhelmina and the pilot's backpack.

And dropped behind a pile of rubble.

It was a slight sound. A sound that was out of rhythm with the jungle.

Carter listened.

Someone was creeping up on the village.

EIGHTEEN

In the heat of midday, the jungle clicks like a clock. It has a beat—wings flapping the air, birds calling, monkeys chattering, insects roaming, fish jumping.

Carter listened for the out-of-sync sounds of the stalker in the jungle.

The stalker was good—patient and quiet—and inexorably closing in on the village.

Carter wiped the sweat from his face. He pulled on the backpack. Wilhelmina in hand, he turned over onto his belly and crawled toward the sounds.

The stalker was turning, skirting the village.

Carter followed, pausing behind the rubble of a hut.

The stalker continued slowly, quietly in the jungle.

Footsteps suddenly dashed behind the hospital.

The stalker was on hard dirt now. In the village.

Carter pulled himself on elbows and toes toward the hospital.

Carter couldn't see him.

Then a flash of camouflage colors.

Feet running around the hospital compound.

A bullet whined above Carter's head and settled in a baobob tree behind.

The stalker was behind another hut.

Carter crawled toward him.

Watching.

Waiting for something to shoot at.

A grenade fell six feet behind Carter.

It was live.

Carter jumped up and hefted the grenade back at the hut.

Bullets whined past Carter as he dove behind the hospital.

The grenade exploded above the hut, shooting debris in all directions.

Silence.

Carter took out his striated tape. He wrapped it around a splintered board. With that in one hand and Wilhelmina in the other, he crawled around the hospital wreckage and toward the hut next to where the stalker had been.

Carter heard the movement. As he'd expected, the stalker was there now.

Circling.

Carter waited. Listened.

Catlike footsteps.

Carter leaped to his feet. Ran his thumb over the tape's striations. Threw the burning board over the hut, behind the stalker.

Surprised, the stalker moved away from the burning missile.

Carter met him, Wilhelmina raised.

"Elena!"

Her Luger pointed at Carter's heart.

His was pointed at hers.

A standoff.

He grinned into her astonished, dirty face.

"I was hoping it was you," he said. "Good technique."

"You're not so bad, either, Nick," she said.

"Thought you'd lost me, didn't you?"

She looked around, hesitating. Then she smiled at him.

"I think, N3, that this is a problem for both our countries."

Carter nodded.

"I had the same idea," he said, "or I might have had a shot at you."

They lowered their guns and laughed.

"We'll never know for sure who's better, will we?" she said.

They stood at the edge of the smoldering, destroyed village and grinned at each other in silent salute.

NINETEEN

Nick Carter and Elena Markova found cooked meat hanging from a village pole, cold millet patties, and fresh spring water in a gourd beside a dung cooking fire. They sat in the shade on large stones overlooking the river and ate the greasy food that tasted like a feast. Their backpacks were behind them. Neither of them wanted to look at the village and the death it contained, so they stared into the river that ran clear and cold over multicolored pebbles just beyond their feet.

"We are the most vicious of all hunters," Elena remarked.

"Killing our own kind for the love of killing."

"The most vicious of hunters, and the most astute of prey," she added.

"I couldn've taken you," Carter said. "I exercised self-control."

"Hah!"

"*You* exercised ignorance." Carter smiled.

"How'd you find me?"

"Simple deduction."

"You knew about the Egyptian," Elena accused. They both laughed.

"Obviously," Carter said, "we both knew."

"Phillips," Elena said. "That rat."

"Not in his eyes. He's only out to make a buck."

"Despicable, nevertheless."

"Agreed. But useful from time to time."

"Then you know about the Mahdi business?" Elena asked.

Carter nodded and finished his millet patty.

"Interesting, isn't it," Carter said and wiped his fingers on his trousers, "how bad food tastes good when you're hungry?"

"And Nyala. You know about that, too?"

"Phillips sold the whole package to Hawk," Carter said.

"The Mahdi is supposed to rid the world of evil," Elena said grimly and shook her head. "If there's a Mahdi behind all these coups, one wonders what his definition of evil is."

"There was a Mahdist revolt in the Sudan in the late 1800s," Carter said and picked up the cooked meat. He tasted it. Probably antelope. "The revolt was led by Mohammed Ahmed. He announced himself the Mahdi around 1880. He and his troops killed General Gordon when they captured Khartoum from the British. A nasty bloodletting. The Mahdists fought on until they won complete control of a large part of the Sudan. Just an example—violence seems integral to the history of Mahdist revolts."

"The question is, is this another Mahdi revolution we're dealing with?"

"Looks like it."

Elena Markova chewed thoughtfully. She wore a camouflage shirt tucked untidily into oversize camouflage pants. Her face and hands were streaked with dirt. Her blond hair was pushed back, held with clips, the hair a wild halo around her dirty model's face. Carter thought she had never looked more beautiful.

"How'd you get out of that jet?" Carter inquired and ate.

"It wasn't easy. Thought I was dead for sure. I didn't have time to bail out, so I took it in as best I could. There was a moment before the explosion. I got out and ran. Tripped over a tree root. I went down behind the tree just as the engine exploded." She looked into the river. Water hyacinths made clusters of green and white. "Lucky for me," she said solemnly.

"Not luck. You handled it well."

She shrugged.

"Part of the job?" he suggested.

"As you well know."

They finished their meal and leaned back. The stench from the village was carried downwind now by a breeze from across the river. Carter knew that Elena had recognized the futility of trying to chase on foot the troops in their vehicles. If they couldn't chase them, they would have to outwit them. Carter and Elena would have to make plans soon.

She was restless. He turned to watch her as her eyes roved over the gray-brown river.

"I would like to make love, Nick," Elena said simply. "I thought about enticing you . . ." She glanced at him from the corners of her eyes.

"But what happened in the village troubles you," Carter said. "I don't like it either. A reminder of mankind's ability to use hate disguised by a cause."

"Funny how it makes me want you," she said.

He kissed her, her mouth throbbing against his.

They moved apart.

"It wouldn't work," he said.

"I know," she said and threw her head back to gaze at the clear blue sky.

He held her hand.

He wanted her.

She turned and smiled at him.

"I never learned to cook," she said. "Mother worked in that bakery, but she never taught me to cook anything. I suppose I didn't want to learn. We went to the ballet and to the theater and to visit Lenin's tomb. She encouraged me to do well in school, to get a government job. She thought that once I was grown there'd be plenty of time to learn how to cook and take care of an apartment. Now, every once in a while, the urge comes over me to make a nest—learn to cook, marry, have babies. Then I'd take my children to all the places I went as a child and, in a way, I could be a child again. Sometimes I think I would like that . . . to be a child again.''

Carter squeezed her hand.

"But then," she continued, her face somber, "this is the way I live now. From moment to moment, job to job. It seems more important.''

"When I thought you'd died," Carter said, "it left an empty place in me.''

"Thank you," Elena said softly.

They sat by the edge of the river, listening to jungle and river sounds, as the sun slowly made its way into the afternoon sky. Mosquitoes would soon be out in force.

"You know about the Riyadh coup?" Carter asked her.

"Oddly inconclusive, like al-Barzani's coup in Baghdad," Elena said. "The rebels start out powerfully with surprise, and then there's no clear-cut victory or defeat.''

Carter nodded.

"Blenkochev is puzzled . . . and worried.''

"Hawk is far from elated.''

"I could never get any specific information at al-Barzani's headquarters. Lots of rumors. Lots of activity and big speeches. But try to pin anyone down about actual plans . . . well, either they didn't have any or that operation had the best security I've seen outside Russia.''

Carter smiled.

"You're bragging," he said.

"Only a little.''

She twined her fingers through his, and warmth spread up his arm. He looked across into the forested jungle that lined the opposite riverbank.

"I wonder just how many sides Phillips is on," Carter mused.

"As many as will pay him.''

"He probably planned to hand the Egyptian Farouk over to whoever got here first.''

"Phillips must be alive still," Elena said.

"And not far away. He doesn't trust any of us, just like we don't trust him."

"He lives nearby, doesn't he?"

Nick Carter and Elena Markova stared at one another. The time had come to make plans, to do their part to stop the fanatic Muslim extremists who had already caused so much death.

TWENTY

While Elena Markova carried her backpack into the forest, Nick Carter moved to the center of the Dinka village. The villagers as well as other tribes in the region are called Nilotes because of their association with the Nile. He glanced at the long slender bodies steaming in the afternoon sun and shook his head. The Dinkas are farmers and herders, the kind who welcome a hospital and the benefits it brings to Nilotes of all tribes.

Carter squatted in the center of the village, the AXE "recorder" radio on his knee. He didn't turn it on.

In the forest, Elena would be doing the same.

"AXE," Carter said into the radio. "Calling AXE. This is N3 calling AXE."

He lit a cigarette.

"N3 calling AXE. Come in, please."

He smoked the cigarette and talked into the unresponsive radio.

He talked for a long time, a fake call similar to the one Elena would be making, trying to reach their home bases.

At last Carter sat back, shaking his head, apparently frustrated that he couldn't get through.

He lit another cigarette, heard the soft sounds behind him.

He dragged on the cigarette.

Waiting.

She was on him like a panther.

Her arm tight against his throat, pulling him back, choking him.

118

He broke the grip and flipped her over his head and onto her back in the dust in front of him.

Elena scrambled to her feet, a knife in her hand. It glinted in the hot sun.

He let her kick Wilhelmina away.

As she turned back to him, he aimed a foot at the knife.

Deliberately missed.

She grinned evilly, enjoying herself.

They circled one another, arms outstretched, shoulders hunched.

Carter kicked the air again.

Elena moved in.

Jammed the knife up, alongside his side in the air, hidden by their close bodies from anyone's sight.

He moaned and slumped.

She pushed him down.

The victor, she leaned over him and clandestinely smeared soft red lipstick down his face and over his side. It would be blood from a distance.

She stood over him.

"Die here, fool!" she shouted, triumphant. "The sun will cook you, and the flies will eat you!"

She wiped her clean knife on her camouflage pants and stalked west, following the tracks the soldiers had made. She was a jaunty figure, her backpack bouncing with each swinging stride.

Carter closed his eyes and moaned. Sweat dripped down his face. The flies swarming over nearby bodies sounded as loud as bees. Soon they would wonder about him.

He rolled over and crawled feebly, dragging the backpack and stopping often, toward a hut that was only half collapsed.

Inside the hut he stretched in a corner smelling of thatch and earth. He groaned loudly and closed his eyes. The heat was stifling.

Again, he waited.

And considered the question of why the renegade Muslims were in the Sudan.

The country's name comes from the medieval term *Bilad as Sudan*, which means "land of the blacks." The Sudan, the largest country in Africa, is an amalgamation of Arabs and Africans: in the north, mostly Muslim Arabs, and in the south, mostly Christian and animist blacks with more than a hundred tribes of different ethnic backgrounds. The Sudan is a peaceful country, working diligently to enter the twentieth century. To achieve its goal of becoming the breadbasket of the Arab world, the government invites companies from the United States to explore for oil and to establish factories to process sugar cane and cotton. The Sudan causes few political problems, content to offer sanctuary to refugees from such war-torn countries as Zaire. The Sudan's biggest political fear, though, is—.

The voice was distant but close enough to be in the village.

A male voice, approaching Carter's hut.

"Two agents. American and Soviet," the voice said as if reporting. "The Soviet agent may have killed the American. Probably to get a head start. . . . Don't be testy—the American is one less you'll have to worry about later."

Carter recognized the slight Canadian accent.

Phillips.

"Of course!" Phillips continued in Arabic. "You're not dealing with an idiot. Wish I could say the same about your people."

Phillips stood in the dim hut's doorway, waiting for his eyes to adjust.

"He's right here," Phillips said, stepping in. "I'll check."

Carter lunged across the room, his chest tight with rage.

"He's alive!" Phillips shouted into the radio. "It's Nick—"

Carter tackled Phillips, shoving him out of the hut and into the compound.

Phillips chopped a steel-hard hand against Carter's neck, twisted, and tried to bring a knee up into Carter's groin.

Carter dropped his weight onto the wily Canadian, forcing him to the ground.

Phillips punched Carter's jaw, a glancing blow that smeared across Elena's lipstick.

Carter wanted to kill Phillips.

But Carter was a professional. He needed Phillips.

Carter took a deep breath and pinned the struggling Phillips down. He sat on the heaving chest and pushed the thin muscular arms beneath his own incredibly strong legs.

"Need any help?" Elena Markova said sweetly from behind.

"You're late."

Carter sat up, his hands free, and stared down at the twisting, swearing Phillips.

She walked around to where she could see Phillips.

"A pretty sight."

Phillips opened his mouth to complain.

Carter smashed a fist into Phillips's jaw.

For a moment, Phillips looked frustrated. Then he went limp and closed his eyes.

"Damn fine work, N3," Elena commented.

"A mere bagatelle," Carter said modestly.

As Elena laughed, remembering, Carter got up and dusted himself off.

"You look like you've been to a whorehouse," Elena said, still laughing. "Filthy—and lipstick all over you."

"It was a pleasure," Carter replied with a grin.

Elena kissed him.

"I know your kind," she said, teasing. Then she looked at him closely.

Carter stared back.

"Don't worry," she said seriously, "one of us will get to kill him sooner or later."

TWENTY-ONE

Carter and Elena retrieved their backpacks and Phillips's radio and dragged Phillips into the shade of a large mahogany tree. They tied Phillips to the tree, then sat beside him, waiting for him to regain consciousness.

"What do you think that is?" Elena said, nodding at a forge and a pile of scrap metal.

"Blacksmith forge," Carter said. "Those springs are probably from an old Land-Rover. Dinkas make spears, knives, and hoes from them."

"And they keep—or kept—cattle, too," Elena said. "Obviously very proud of them, each with its own tether and stake."

Carter nodded.

"Workers from USAID have been trying to teach the Dinkas to use their cattle to plow, but the cow and ox are sacred here," he said. "When a Dinka boy enters adulthood, he takes a new name from a bull calf in his father's herd. With cattle, he pays taxes and buys staples. And, when he courts, he takes his cow along to show his girl how splendid and wealthy he is." Carter smiled. "Trying to get a Dinka to use his ox to plow is like trying to get a European to use his Rolls-Royce to mulch his lawn."

"All people hold onto the past," Elena said. "In Siberia, shoppers carry their milk home frozen solid in a paper bag. They really don't have to do that, but it's a custom and they like it."

"I didn't know anyone liked anything about Siberia," Carter teased.

"Some do," Elena said seriously. "And that gives me an idea."

She walked across the compound to the stack of new spears beside the blacksmith's forge. The natives hadn't had time to get weapons before the soldiers attacked. She picked up the spears, brought them to the shade of the mahogany tree, and stuck them in the dirt in a semicircle around Phillips. They stood at sharp angles, pointing at Phillips's chest.

"What do you think?" Elena asked.

"A work of art."

"Thanks. I thought so."

She sat beside Carter again, and he put an arm around her. She slapped a mosquito on her forearm, grimaced, pulled down her sleeves, and buttoned them at the wrists.

"There are sixty-three varieties of mosquitoes along the Nile," she commented.

"Which kind got you?" Carter asked.

He moved away to get the pilot's backpack.

"Not the kind that carries sleeping sickness, I hope," she said.

"Put this on. U.S. Army surplus mosquito dope. If you can stand the smell, you won't be bitten anymore."

"Thanks."

She slathered the foul-smelling liquid over her face, neck, and hands, then handed the plastic bottle to him. She watched as he put it on.

"I like being held," she said, "even by stinky men, when it's you."

He smiled and again put his arm around her. She moved in his arms like a kitten, soft and purring.

"What's that blasted smell!"

Phillips was awake, staring angrily around.

"Your morals," Carter said.

Elena hooted gleefully. She kicked a spear so that the point landed on Phillips's heart. It went through his cotton shirt, and a small red stain appeared.

"What're you doing!" Phillips shouted, struggling against the ropes that held him stationary to the tree.

"I wonder how good my aim is, Nick," Elena said thoughtfully. "Shall I start at fifty paces and work my way forward?"

She picked up a spear.

"Phillips," Carter said, "I have bad news for you. Elena is angry."

Elena stood up, hoisted the spear, pulled it back over her shoulder, and shot her arm forward toward Phillips's heart as if she were going to throw the spear.

Phillips blanched and tried to duck.

"You can't kill me!"

"Why not?" Elena asked. "You're not exactly Blenkochev's favorite person."

"Or Hawk's," Carter said. "In fact, I believe Hawk has a replacement all picked out for you."

"No one can replace me! No one knows . . ."

Phillips stopped, his thin lips suddenly compressed.

"What's in this for me?" Phillips asked cagily.

"Your life, maybe," Carter said.

"If you're lucky," Elena added, rubbing the spear affectionately.

A freebooter like Phillips avoids being a hero. It is inefficient, and he might not live to spend his savings. That would go against everything he believes in. Everything he has lived for.

"Are you working for the troops that demolished this village?" Carter asked quietly.

Phillips sighed and looked at the semicircle of spears pointing at him.

"They didn't pay me nearly enough."

"But you're working for them?" Elena said.

"Why else would I be here?"

Carter nodded. "Did you hit all the military wavelengths until you found a customer?"

"All I had to do was mention a vanished Egyptian, and they jumped," Phillips said haughtily. "They paid, and I told them where to find him."

"Obviously closer to begin with than we were," Elena said.

"And you were still in contact with them when you came back into the village," Carter said. "You were selling Elena and me to them."

Phillips shrugged.

Elena rubbed the edge of the sharp spear against the stubble on Phillips's cheek. He flinched but stared straight at her. He was a proud man, hardened into insensitivity to pain or fear.

"Who were they?" Carter asked, his voice soft.

Phillips was insensitive, but he knew that as long as he talked, he would live. Loyalty had no meaning for him.

"All I know is that they looked like regular Sudanese troops. Probably had some U.S. training. There were advisers with them."

"U.S. advisers?" Elena asked. She looked at Carter. "Cooley?"

"Maybe," Carter said.

"But why would regular Sudanese troops and American advisers want to murder an Egyptian official?" Elena wondered.

"Don't know and don't care," Phillips said.

"It's the Mahdi business," Carter responded. "The connections are there. We need to know the extent of it."

There was a sudden blaring from the forest.

A series of electronic squawks.

Carter and Elena dropped to the ground.

Picked up their Lugers.

Swiveled toward the sound.

"I think I can tell you all about it, Killmaster!" A loud voice amplified by an electronic bullhorn rattled the forest. "They're renegade Sudanese troops, and the Day of the Mahdi is the master plan of Islamic renegades to take over the entire Arab world!"

TWENTY-TWO

The forest was silent. Nick Carter and Elena Markova lay stretched flat, their Lugers pointed steadily toward the forest from where the amplified voice had come. Their eyes scanned the thick trees and vegetation. A parrot suddenly streaked across the compound, frightened into flight.

"Say one word," Carter warned Phillips in a whisper, "and you're dead."

"How did they hear us?" Elena wanted to know.

Carter picked up Phillips's radio.

"Transmitter's still on."

Elena grimaced and nodded as Carter turned it off.

"Who the hell are you?" Carter shouted into the trees.

The voice boomed with a long, growling laugh.

"We knew better than to try to get any closer to you, N3," the voice said. "This is Brigadier General T.S. Taylor, Special Forces, antiterrorist, with one platoon of the best. Sent by direct order of the President to give you a hand. May we come in?"

Phillips groaned.

"What do you think?" Elena asked.

Carter considered.

"How did you or the President know where I was, Taylor?" Carter shouted.

"No problem," the voice responded. "David Hawk called for help. You can check on me. I'm sure you have ways."

Carter retrieved the radio that looked like a tape cassette from the pilot's backpack.

"Give us a few minutes," Carter shouted.

"Done!"

Carter punched the buttons on the recorder that would connect him with the AXE computer. He adjusted the radio so Elena could hear as well.

"Yes, N3," the computer purred in her sexy voice. "how may I serve you?"

"The marvels of American technology?"

"One of Hawk's jokes," Carter said gruffly.

"You men!"

Carter ignored her.

"Do you have a record on Brigadier General T.S. Taylor?" Carter asked the computer.

"Of course, N3," the computer said, her voice tinged with hurt. "Would you like a readout?"

"Yes."

"I only wanted to be sure," the computer said contritely. "Brigadier General Thackery Simpson Taylor, forty-five, is with Special Forces on detached service awaiting direct orders from the Secretary of Defense and/or the President. He was a combat commander in the Green Berets in Vietnam and led paratroopers into the Grenada conflict. He is the great-great-grandson of Zachary Taylor and the great-grandson of the fire-eating Confederate General Richard Taylor. Currently, Brigadier General T.S. Taylor is stationed in Washington, D.C. His assignment is to stay in readiness to go anywhere in the world with a Special Forces unit." The computer voice paused. "I have his immediate secret location. Would you like it, N3?"

"It'd be a help."

"I hoped so, sir," the computer said politely. "The President's office has ordered him to the southern Sudan, Top Secret assignment, Code N-Zero."

"N-Zero is Hawk," Elena said helpfully.

"You Russian spies do get around," Carter muttered.

"He's authentic, but what about me?" Elena asked.

"It's not the first time that the United States and Russia have worked together."

"I hope it's not the last," Elena said, her eyes worried, "for me."

Carter touched her arm and spoke into the computer. "Thanks. You've been a doll."

"Farewell, N3. It's always a pleasure to serve you."

Carter shook his head and turned off the fake cassette recorder.

"Okay, General," Carter shouted into the forest, "come on in!"

General T.S. Taylor was about five-foot-nine, dressed from head to toe in tailored, slim-fitting camouflage fatigues. He wore custom-made jump boots complete with a knife in the right boot, a red, English paratroop beret on his bald head, bandoliers of ammunition across his chest, an ivory-handled pistol at his belt, and an automatic rifle cradled in his arms, patrol style. He walked with a spring, as if always ready to fight, his bone-hard body tight with anticipation, his eagle eyes roaming the compound. He loved his work.

Behind him came other troopers, all dressed similarly but without his custom-made, privileged trappings. The troops knew their jobs. They spread through the village, looking for life and danger.

"Welcome to the Sudan, General," Carter said.

Taylor saluted Carter, but his eyes were on Elena and Phillips, who was still tied to the tree. He nodded curtly at Carter and pointed to Elena and Phillips.

"Them?"

"The lady and I are on the same assignment, General," Carter said and smiled. "Under the circumstances, we agreed to join forces."

Taylor nodded.

"CIA or British?"

"KGB," Carter said, keeping a straight face.

Taylor's eyes went empty, but again he nodded.

Behind him, some of his soldiers were muttering over the corpses of the Dinkas, commenting on the ornamental facial scars peculiar to the tribe.

"And him?" Taylor asked.

"Phillips. A local agent," Carter said, "for whichever side pays last or best or both."

"He looks it," Taylor said.

Phillips stared ahead, his face expressionless.

Taylor considered Carter, and looked him up and down, obviously not pleased by the Killmaster's height and physique. Taylor scowled.

"Take Phillips with us?"

"Take him or kill him," Carter said. "Leave him and we're dead."

"Take him where, General?" Elena asked.

The worry was gone from her face. Now she wore the professional mask that covered all emotions. She was on the alert and would be until the situation proved safe.

"Farouk dead?" the general countered.

"Killed by Sudanese troops with American advisers, it appears," Carter said.

"Thought so," Taylor said. "We go after the attackers, of course. They came from somewhere and they'll go back to somewhere. We picked up their trail about three miles away, heading northwest."

"Heading to a town called Nyala?" Carter asked.

The general smiled all around, pleased at the adventures that awaited him. His polished teeth shone in the lowering sun. He would be ferocious and brave, this general.

"Let's go get 'em!" he said and rubbed his hands together.

TWENTY-THREE

The U.S. Army trucks and jeeps painted in the green-and-brown stripes of camouflage colors stretched out over the dusty track; road is seldom an appropriate term in rural Sudan. The track was a rough trail raised above what was a swampy marsh during the Sudan's rainy season. To the north were the low, rolling Nuba Mountains, as invisible because of distance as the new Jonglei Canal was to the south.

Nick Carter, Elena Markova, General Taylor, and the others drove through a flat savanna country of acacias, tall grasses, and open forests, leaving behind the off-and-on swampy areas around the southern White Nile that is called the Sudd, which, during the rainy season, extend to an area as large as Maine. The travelers were hot and uncomfortable. Their clothes stuck to them like tar paper. Their throats were dust-coated, and no amount of water could slake their thirsts.

After two hours of the rough, bouncing drive, they stopped to make camp. Traveling in the Sudan's back country was dangerous enough even when there was light.

They left the vehicles on the track and moved to a packed-down spot in the vast yellow grasslands. Not far away were dome-shaped huts that resembled huge haystacks of thatch. A few cattle grazed nearby in the twilight.

A Nilote with skin the blue-black color of eggplant walked proudly toward them, a cattle tether in his hand, as if interrupted at work, and a hard hat on his head.

"Nuer," Carter said to Elena.

"How can you tell?"

"Tribal markings," Carter explained.

The soldiers got out sleeping bags and opened C rations. A sergeant directed some of them to guard the vehicles, others to dig a latrine. Two crawled under the jeeps and trucks, looking for cracked axles or other breakdowns that could happen on the rugged track.

"General," Carter called, "we've got a visitor."

Taylor looked up, as neatly pressed as ever, although large circles of sweat now decorated his underarms.

"Who?"

"A local businessman," Carter said and grinned.

Taylor dusted his hands, pointed at a corner of his sleeping bag that wasn't quite right, and left his aide to finish. Not far away, Phillips sat, his wrists tied, a soldier standing guard beside him. As Taylor walked to Carter and Elena, he took out a large white handkerchief and patted his square-jawed face.

"Why?"

"Courtesy call, I expect," Carter said.

"Okay. Let's get it over with."

The Nuer stood in front of them.

"*Marissa?*" the Nuer said. "Do you have beer?" He smiled charmingly. "It is time to celebrate. My people are not yet here, but you are."

"What'd he say?" Taylor asked Carter.

Carter translated the dialect, and Taylor frowned.

"Beer!" Taylor spat and walked away.

The Nuer looked innocently from Carter to Elena and back again.

"No beer? I am indeed thirsty, aren't you?"

"Just a moment," Elena said. "I think I can help."

The Nuer watched Elena as she swung away.

"Been here long?" Carter asked.

"Three days," the Nuer replied. "I think of *Maneh*, God, and pray the people come soon."

The Nuer continued to watch Elena as she walked to a cluster of soldiers.

The Nuers, like the Dinkas, are a cattle-keeping people who move between plains and swamps with the seasons. Isolated for centuries, the Nuers are now being exposed to modern-day commerce.

"I like your hat," Carter said.

The Nuer nodded, pleased.

"Yes. Very good. I worked rigs for the Chevron Oil Company near Bahr al-Ghazal."

"Is that why you have so many cattle?"

"Very rich now. *Maneh* watches and blesses me."

The Nuer's smile spread wide, and he turned to gesture at the cattle grazing in the yellow grasslands beside the thatched huts.

Elena brought back three Camel beers. The Nuer dropped his cattle tether over his shoulder and clapped his hands.

"*Marissa!*"

They squatted on the compacted grass and drank. The Nuer's name was Simon. He had left his family at their village.

"Your decorations are very fine," Elena said to him, running her fingers across her forehead to imitate the six lines of scars across Simon's.

"If my head is not cut," Simon said of the male puberty rite, "the men can beat me, I can cry. If it is cut, then they can beat me and even kill me, but I cannot cry. How could I cry?" He raised his shoulders and shrugged. "It is just a woman who can cry. You become a man."

"You must be very brave," Elena said.

Simon stared thoughtfully at her.

"You are pale," Simon said at last. "Are you healthy?"

Elena smiled and glanced at Carter. Her nose and cheeks were sunburned. She looked like a schoolgirl after a day at the beach.

"Ask him," she said, indicating Carter.

"Is she healthy?" Simon asked Carter, his face serious with concern.

Elena watched, amused.

"Most definitely," Carter said. "Very healthy."

Simon nodded. "Good. It is important for a woman to be healthy and have many babies."

"Just what I was saying," Elena said and laughed.

They sat in their small circle as the sun went down over the savanna, talking and making jokes. At last, as the beer was gone and the cattle were lowing, the Nuer stood up to leave.

"I thank you," he said. "That was good."

"I'm surprised no one else stopped here," Carter said, standing. "Perhaps, though, you have seen others go by?"

The Nuer nodded.

"Very fast. Much dust."

"Who were they?" Elena asked.

"Soldiers." Simon shrugged.

"What kind of soldiers?"

"Like you. Trucks. But also our soldiers."

"Did they have any markings? Any way to identify them as different?" Elena asked.

"Perhaps there were signs on the vehicles?" Carter added.

Simon's eyes got big as he remembered.

"A strange flag. Ours, but no green . . ." He made a triangle of his fingers. "On one jeep."

"Red, white, and black stripes only?" Carter asked.

"Yes. That is right."

"Libya," Elena said and looked at Carter.

"Iraq, Iran, Saudi Arabia, and now Libya," Carter said thoughtfully.

"I must go," Simon said. He shook hands firmly with Carter.

Elena extended her hand. Simon looked at it, then took it.

"Very excellent *marissa*!" He pumped her hand and disappeared into the darkening savanna.

"I've made a conquest," Elena said lightly.

"It could be stolen," Carter said.

"My conquest?"

"The jeep with Libyan markings. The Sudanese could have stolen a Libyan jeep. Libya is on the Sudan's northwest border. Convenient."

Elena turned away and walked into the camp to find her sleeping bag. The soldiers' electric lanterns made streams of light in the night, and Carter followed her over the compressed grass.

"I know what you're thinking," she said as she sat on her sleeping bag.

In the dimness, Carter saw her stare at her boots. She knocked the toes together.

"Wish I could sleep without these damned things."

"At least change your socks," he said. "It'll help."

Elena nodded and reached into her backpack. She and Carter took off their boots and put on clean, dry socks, and then the boots again. They laid the old socks out to dry, to be worn the next night if necessary. They would sleep on top of their sleeping bags because of the heat, and to sleep without boots was to risk insect and viper bites, and cut feet when they got up. They put on more insect repellent.

"What am I thinking?" Carter said.

"That Libya is working with Russian arms and Russian, East German, and Cuban experts. That Iraq is, too. That it may be in the best interests of Russia—particularly if Libya is involved—to back off and let the Muslims do their worst."

"The thought had crossed my mind." Carter took out his cigarette case and offered a cigarette to Elena.

She took one, and he lit it and his.

"Sudan and Saudi Arabia create the same problem for me," she said. "They're pro-American. If the Sudan is behind all this, and it might be, then—well—maybe I should call in and get the hell out of here, back to my people."

"You sound like Simon—'my people' and 'the people.'"

"Our countries . . . or tribe, in his case. The sense of family and belonging and responsibility that all countries call patriotism. I am and always will be a Russian."

"I know."

"And you will always be an American. Our countries first, before personal wants . . . or needs."

They smoked and listened to the brittle sounds of flying and creeping insects as, one by one, the soldiers turned off their lanterns. Carter and Elena put out their cigarettes.

"I can't even hold your hand now," Elena said as she lay on her sleeping bag. "It all feels wrong."

Carter stretched on his bag, the soft down and grasses beneath making a comfortable cushion, much more comfortable than many places he had slept, but he was restless. He moved on the bag, trying to find a place to settle. At last, exhausted, he simply stopped moving and willed himself to relax.

Finally he spoke.

"I trust you, Elena. I know what you believe in, and I can understand it. I respect your professional integrity. That's more than I can say of most people I meet."

Carter heard Elena turn on her side. He felt her eyes on him.

"You will watch me, and I will watch you," she said.

"The way it has to be," he said.

TWENTY-FOUR

Nick Carter awoke to a gray dawn and the stirrings of the camp. In the distance, the Nuer sat beside his dung fire, rubbing his eyes, squatting like a beetle. And beside Carter, Elena Markova and her sleeping bag were gone, the bag tied up neatly beside a jeep different from the one they had ridden in together the day before.

She was nowhere in sight.

Carter peed, rinsed his mouth, picked up a cup of coffee from a corporal with a collapsible stove and two constantly full pots on it, and walked away from camp. He sat cross-legged, his radio on his lap. He made the adjustments to link in directly to Hawk's private line at AXE.

And turned the radio on.

There was no sound.

He pushed the buttons, off and on, off and on.

Nothing.

He needed to talk to Hawk.

Using his pocketknife, he unscrewed the radio's top panel. With luck, some wire would be obviously loose and he could simply tighten it. The radio had had enough jouncing the day before to shake loose several wires. He took off the top and looked inside. Wires and chips and clips, colorful and complicated, and all thoroughly connected. It was an electronic genius's playbox, and Carter wasn't an electronic genius. He stared with dismay at the radio's innards, at last putting the case back together.

He walked back to camp.

Found a corporal with a radioman's patch.

136

"I need to make a call to Washington," Carter said. "Top Secret clearance."

"Sorry."

The radioman had a blond crewcut and a freckled, blunt nose. He was cleaning the radio, using a small plastic bottle of household wax and an old pair of undershorts.

"No one makes calls out," the radioman continued. "General's orders."

Carter turned and marched to the general's sleeping area. General Taylor was sitting on a campstool, drinking coffee and talking with Phillips. Phillips stood before him, hands clasped behind his back, narrow face attentive and almost smiling.

"How much did you offer him, General?" Carter inquired as he walked up.

"What?"

"Phillips never looks this happy unless money is involved," Carter said.

"I'm a practical man," Phillips said, scowling. "Not a jerk-ass sentimental romantic like you."

"You always know where you stand with Phillips," Carter said to the general. "Well, how much did you pay him? And for what?"

The general examined his short, tidy fingernails.

"I paid him his life," the general said and looked up, "in exchange for good behavior. He may be useful later. In any case, I'm not prepared to kill him in cold blood, nor am I prepared to waste a soldier to watch him."

"He's free then?"

Carter stared at Phillips, and Phillips smirked in return.

"Until I rescind those orders, yes."

"Free as a bird!" Phillips chortled.

"I hope you don't regret that decision," Carter said to the general.

General Taylor shrugged and drank his coffee.

"You can go now, Phillips," Taylor said and smacked his lips. "Keep your nose clean."

Once Phillips was out of earshot, heading for the coffee pots, Carter spoke.

"I need to call AXE," he said. "My radio's out. I'll have to use yours."

The general tipped his cup and finished the coffee.

"Sorry. No-can-do."

The general stood, stretched his arms above his head, then bent at the waist to touch his toes.

"Hawk expects regular reports from me," Carter said. "The President expects reports from Hawk."

The general clasped his hands behind his head and swiveled, stretching his back muscles. Beads of sweat popped out on his face.

"Radio silence," the general said, forcing air in and out of his lungs. "President's orders," he huffed.

The general did jumping jacks in his immaculate uniform, his face drenched in sweat, his eyes glowing. At last he stopped and reached out his right hand. An aide appeared from nowhere to lay a folded white towel in the hand. The general shook out the towel and buried his wet face in it. He tossed it at the aide.

"Now, son," the general said, throwing an arm up over Carter's shoulder to usher him toward the trucks and jeeps, "take it easy. You can give your report to me. I have as much authority as Hawk. Maybe more."

"*My* orders are to report only to Hawk."

"I saved you, boy," the general said. "Don't you think you can trust me?"

Carter stared into the faded blue eyes that would never see as many campaigns as the general dreamed of, at the smooth cheeks shaved so close that the pores looked empty, at the jaw muscles working under the ears as the general waited for Carter to give the correct response.

"No reason not to," Carter said.

The general clapped Carter on the back.

"Good, son. And don't you worry about Phillips. He's a Canuck. Good, sturdy stock up there. Reliable as long as they're not pansy French or English. If you want to keep your eye on someone, watch that Commie broad of yours. Wouldn't trust her to knit me a scarf. Probably strangle me with it!" He hit Carter's back. "Great in bed! There you can keep 'em pinned down!"

"On the contrary," Carter said stiffly, pulling away from the general, "I find Ms. Markova reliable in all ways."

"No offense, boy!" the general said, leaving Carter at the jeep. "Just remember I warned you."

The general strode back through the deserted campground, looked for lost possessions and poor cleanup, then, satisfied, returned to the lead jeep that flew small American flags on both front fenders.

General Taylor stood up in the back seat, turned to survey the ragged line of vehicles, waved his arm in a large circle, and shouted.

"Roll 'em out!"

Motors roared and choked and roared again. The general's driver led off, followed by other jeeps and the trucks carrying the troops.

A slight breeze ruffled the tall savanna grasses. The breeze was already hot, a harbinger of the day's coming temperatures. They drove past giraffe bones piled in a heap, the neck vertebrae having been stacked neatly in a monument. Horned hartebeests, reedbucks, and gazelles fled across the plains even before the vehicles came in sight. Carter and the soldiers watched the animals' tails bouncing into the golden brown horizon.

The soldiers all carried automatic rifles, and machine guns were mounted at the backs of the jeeps, World War II-fashion. The men had inspected all the arms and ammunition first thing, before the sun was full upon the savanna. Then they had checked the liters of diesel fuel, oil, water, and the mechanics' spare parts. By the time the platoon had left, all supplies were accounted for and tied down, except for the personal supplies that Elena and Carter carried. Those, they were responsible for.

The air smelled of dust and heat. Talking as well as breathing seemed impossible. They watched the countryside. Occasionally a thorn tree stood in solitary magnificence, the sunlight so bright that the tree appeared to be black. They saw mongooses, weaverbirds, and numerous small birds that darted among the grasses looking for insects.

Elena was in another jeep, sitting with the radioman, a corporal, and the coffee-maker. Her blond hair had grown stiff with sweat and dust. At the last stop, the general had gallantly given her his neck scarf to cover it. Now she looked as if all she needed was a station wagon to make her look like a suburban housewife on the way to the beauty parlor.

Carter had not talked to her since last night. She was ignoring him, and the general had noticed.

Every forty miles or so, the caravan stopped to check radiators and to relieve the bouncing of the passengers' bones. They were moving more and more away from water and into the wasteland of the Sudan's savannas that wavered in the day's heat. Worried about dehydration, they kept themselves fully clothed and drank water.

By the time they reached their third stop of the day, Carter's head ached and his teeth felt loose. He got out and stood beside the jeep, stretched, and lit a cigarette. Just standing up made him feel better. He drank deeply from his canteen.

Elena walked by him, staring solemnly.

He had nothing to say.

She shrugged and joined the general.

"Nice piece of ass, that," Phillips said, sidling up to Carter. "Wouldn't mind a bite of it." He laughed shortly. "Nourishing." He bared his teeth.

Carter threw his cigarette into the track rut and smashed it with his heel.

"One more word about her, Phillips, and I'll kill you."

Carter walked away, hearing Phillips's barking laugh behind him. Phillips was alive not because the general said he could live, but because Carter wasn't sure yet how he fit into the Day of the Mahdi. This time Carter intended to have all the answers for Hawk, and now Phillips would keep his mouth shut about Elena Markova for a while.

Carter joined the general and Elena. From the intense look on her beautiful face, she was asking him questions, trying to convince him to answer. The general was thinking his own thoughts, humoring her for reasons of his own—personal reasons. When Elena saw Carter approaching, she leaned away from the general and quit talking.

"Don't know why a nice little girl like you works as a spy." General Taylor was saying, his eyes transfixed on the dirty but exquisite Elena Markova. "If I didn't know you were a godless Russian, I might even get to like you. Maybe persuasion would help." He lifted her chin to look into her eyes. "I'm willing to give it a try . . ."

"You might catch a disease, General," Carter said, smiling grimly at Elena, whose expressionless face could have been made of stone. "Isn't that what you believe— that Russians, and Chinese, and Israelis, and blacks, and all other minorities are disease-ridden, unintelligent, inferior peoples who need to be led by clean, straight-thinking Americans?"

The general dropped his hand from Elena's chin and glared irritably at Carter.

"What?"

"What do you know about the Day of the Mahdi?" Carter demanded. "How extensive is the conspiracy?"

"That!" General Taylor's interest shifted abruptly. "Hawk didn't seem to know. That's why *I'm* here. He got a report from Saudi Arabia that the renegades have drafted plans to conquer Iraq, Iran, Saudi Arabia, Yemen, Oman, Kuwait, Qatar, the Sudan, and Libya. Later, after that's consolidated, they'll take over Egypt, Israel, Jordan, Lebanon, Syria, and any other countries that have enough Muslims to give 'em a reason for 'liberation.' You got that, boy?"

"What about Cooley?"

"Who?"

"Melvin J. Cooley, chairman of the board of Universal Mining and Refining."

"No importance. Heard about the scheme and been trying to get oil rights in advance. Beat the Russkies."

"Just a good businessman, huh?"

"That's about it." The general hiked up his pants and winked at Markova. "Men talk," he explained.

She smiled, big-eyed and innocent. What was she after?

"And why *are* you here, General? Not only to save my hide, I'm sure," Carter said.

"You're sharp. Give you that. It's the Nyala part of the note. We've heard there's something big gonna happen there. Really big. Seems they got kind of standoffs in Saudi Arabia and Iraq. The thing at Nyala's gonna swing it. Information's from a reliable source, and Hawk believed it enough to send me."

"And the Mahdi? Who is the Mahdi?"

"Don't know that there is one in particular. Hotheads calling themselves Mahdi pop up all the time. Could be just a rallying gimmick."

The ring of a small alarm sounded through the general's words. He grunted and pressed his thumb against the side of his watch.

"Time to get moving," he said. "Captain!"

The soldiers and civilians piled back into the hot, dusty vehicles, the general alone with his driver in the lead jeep, Elena Markova next to the blond radioman in another jeep, and Carter following in a third. They drove off into the plodding, endless day.

That night was hot and restless, a wind rubbing scrub tree and bush branches into long, eerie squeaks. Lizards and mice made scurrying noises across the ground. Carter lay on his sleeping bag at the side of the camp, alone. Elena slept far away, also alone, and Phillips was in a third area close to the general. The soldiers were spread out on the bags, silent with sleep. Occasionally, Carter saw the red glows of cigarettes from the two soldiers who guarded the vehicles. The hot, moving air seemed alive in the night, and Carter got up.

He'd slept earlier, but not now. He stared at the twinkling canopy of stars, lit a cigarette, and walked through the camp.

He wasn't sure what had attracted his attention, made him get up.

Maybe it was the soldier's awkward sleeping position.

Maybe it was the blood that made a black void in the night.

Carter stopped and stared around the camp.

Unmoving silence, except for the wind in the scattered scrub.

Carter ground out his cigarette and walked to the soldier. Beside him was the large cube of the platoon's powerful radio.

Carter knelt down.

The blond, freckled, blunt-nosed soldier's intestines had spilled onto his sleeping bag, snakes of black-red, bloody innards pouring from a gaping slash across his white belly.

Carter ran a hand over the soldier's head, finding a lump the size of a hardball that indicated the soldier had been knocked unconscious before he was killed. Then someone had unbuttoned the young man's shirt and trousers, pulled back the clothes, and ceremoniously, quietly, executed him.

The corpse was still warm. The radio was not. But the radio would cool long before a human body would.

Phillips . . . or Elena?

Carter sat on his heels and thought.

Carter had not pursued a call to Hawk—the President ordered radio silence—but that wouldn't stop Phillips or Elena. Elena had her own radio; Phillips had none, his having been confiscated by the general at the Dinka village.

Carter went to awaken the general.

TWENTY-FIVE

The camp streamed with lights from the electric lanterns. Soldiers moved, hushed, and the corporal put on the coffee pots.

The general sat on his campstool, his face stern, holding court.

"Well, Phillips?" the general said.

"Why would I want to radio out?" Phillips said, his hands raised palms up at shoulder height. He was the picture of the aggrieved, innocent accused. "With you, I'm safe. I'll get justice. With the Russians"—his thin lip curled—"who can say?" His voice dropped to a husky, conspiratorial whisper. "Blenkochev is going senile, you know. And the Muslims . . ." He waved a hand in dismissal. "Animals."

The general nodded, understanding and agreeing.

"You could sell our destination," Carter said. "Information is your stock in trade."

Phillips's eyes went wide.

"But I'm along! I could get killed!"

"Sorry," Carter said. "Forgot your cowardice."

Phillips bristled.

"Not cowardice," Phillips said. "Good sense."

Carter shook his head.

"What about you, Killmaster?" the general inquired. "Your radio is broken and you want to call AXE." The general's cool blue eyes appraised Carter.

Carter shrugged.

"The President wants radio silence," Carter said simply.

"I see," the general said. He ran his fingers over the stubble on his chin, felt the bones beneath the tight skin. "And now, Ms. KGB. By the process of elimination, it seems to be you."

Elena's face was hard, her beauty set in granite. For a moment she looked at Carter as if to say *I told you so.*

"Your radio is out, too," General Taylor said, "you tried to talk me into giving you permission to use ours, and you spent the day riding with the radioman to convince him. I know my boys, and he'd maybe string you along, but he sure as hell wouldn't let you use the radio when he's got orders to the contrary. So that leaves you with one big frustrating yen—to report in, and only one means to do it with."

Elena stared in stony silence.

The general stood up and stalked around the civilians and in among the soldiers who were clustered around.

"Any of you boys see an Arab or black sneak into camp tonight?"

"No . . . no . . . no . . ." the soldiers said, some shaking their heads.

"Any of you boys see anyone mucking around where the radioman was sleeping?"

Again, there was a chorus of no's.

"Any of you see anyone up and moving around the last couple of hours?"

Again, none had.

The general nodded and stomped back to his campstool.

"No one from the outside," he said and sat. He crossed his arms. "Guess it must be you, honey." He stared at Elena.

"You're pathetic," Elena said, her head high as she stared down her nose at the general. "I would not be such a fool as to kill one of you and stay. I've not lived at my work for so long by being inept."

"Not inept," General Taylor said. "Desperate." He

nodded at two privates, and they moved to either side of her.

Carter stared at the haughty Russian, then turned to the general.

"You're making a mistake," Carter said. "She kills only when she has to—on orders or for an advantage. It'd do her no good to sacrifice her freedom or life for something she'll be able to report once we're there." Carter watched the general.

The general shifted once, uneasily.

"Don't want any more dead soldiers," he said curtly. "Tie her up. We'll take her with us. Turn her over later."

At daybreak the caravan moved on, leaving behind the golden brown ocean of grass and the grave of the radioman, marked by a buried electronic beacon. The caravan entered what seemed to be another nation, a land of infrequent vegetation and more and more sand that reflected the blistering sun. It was like traveling through an oven. Tempers grew short. New orders forbade even the minimal comfort of a wet bandanna around the neck or a cup of water over the hair. Fuel and water supplies were carefully monitored. The group had two more days of travel, at least.

The caravan occasionally passed market trucks on the tracks. The trucks were the lifelines of the Sudan, the major way people and goods moved about the country. Since the tracks were rough and the trucks often old, the drivers were experience-taught mechanics.

In midafternoon, the caravan stopped to rest and check the vehicles. Thus far, there had been no breakdowns, and the general was determined that the rest of the trip would go as well.

A herd of wild camels galloped across the arid hills in the distance. A vulture flew high against the glassy sky.

Elena got out of her jeep to stand stoically beside it, her wrists tied before her with rope. The soldier who was her guard handed her a canteen. She lifted it and drank eagerly, not losing a drop.

Carter walked to her.

She turned away.

Hawk had sent General Taylor to rescue Carter and to lead the subsequent mission. All organizations had to have people to issue orders and others to follow them. Otherwise there would be anarchy. Carter reminded himself of this as he stood behind Elena's filthy, stubborn . . . small, vulnerable . . . back. Had she killed the soldier?

"How'd your radio break?" Carter asked her at last.

"A cigarette, Jeff?" Elena said to her guard.

The tall, muscular young man with the raw-boned, handsome face took out a pack of Winstons, handed her one, and lit it. The boy didn't smoke, but hungrily watched Elena as she did.

"Mine must've gone out the first day," Carter said. "Too much bouncing on the road, I expect."

Elena turned.

"Is that all you have to say?" she said. "Jeff, I want you to look at the Killmaster here. He's a registered hero. Acts it, doesn't he?"

"Yes, ma'am." The soldier never took his eyes off Elena.

"Elena, stop it," Carter said. "Tell me when it broke."

"Have another plan, N3?" she said bitterly and dragged on the cigarette, the bound hands in front of her face. "The last one worked so well."

"Sometimes you have to ride with events for a while."

Elena's red nail polish was chipping off. She stared at her fingernails angrily.

"Elena," Carter said softly.

She sighed.

"Probably the first day," she said at last, her hands now dangling in front of her. "I used it earlier, after I crawled out of the jet. I didn't turn it on later when we were faking calls to our bases to fool Phillips. And the next morning—the first morning out with your soldiers—it was dead."

The heat the jeep had absorbed throughout the day radiated at them. They couldn't sit on the blistering sand nor lean against the jeep. They kept towels and clothing over the seats so the plastic wouldn't burn them when they returned to the vehicles. Carter wanted to sit down and rest, hold Elena and rest.

"Interesting coincidence," Carter said.

"Is it?" Elena asked.

"I tried my radio that same morning. Dead, too."

She shrugged.

"Probably Phillips," she said. "Just the kind of sneaky thing he'd do. Wouldn't even have to have a reason."

A bus-truck was chugging down the track toward the caravan, passengers leaning out the windows, gazing and pointing.

"I suppose so," Carter said.

Elena and the soldier turned to follow Carter's eyes, watching the mutant vehicle that was a bus body on a truck bed. Distractions in the desert are highly regarded. The tall bus swayed, and the passengers shouted and cheered as it plowed off the track and into the sand to pass the stopped caravan. The bus was like a cage, the windows barred and both doors opening on the same side. It chugged alongside the caravan in the sand, throwing up great brown clouds, and the passengers waved and yelled greetings in Arabic. In the face of such gaiety, even somber soldiers on a mission to save the world have to respond. The soldiers waved slowly, then with more enthusiasm as the beaming bus-truck passengers fairly jumped up and down at the friendly Americans.

Elena noticed the problem first.

"It's listing!" she cried.

The passengers' weight had put the bus off-balance, digging a deeper and deeper rut on the side facing the caravan. The bus driver stood up and leaned out his window through the bars, saw the wheels deep in sand. He shook his head, sat back down, and the bus plowed slowly ahead.

The passengers cheered and waved. The soldiers grinned, shouted, and raised their rifles in salute.

Like an elegant sailing ship with a cracked hull, the bus-truck sank further and further until it was hopelessly off-balance. The passengers noticed and scrambled to the other side, too late but laughing all the while, and the bus-truck keeled onto its side, wheels still turning.

The soldiers ran to the vehicle, but already the passengers were scrambling out between the window bars, carrying baskets of food and fruit and camel skins of water. Their faces streamed with sweat, so they wiped them and reached a hand down through the bars to help the next person out.

The soldiers untied the bleating goats and caged chickens from the roof. Chicken feathers fluttered in the air, and the goats made dashes for freedom, their owners fast behind.

The general stood with his hands on his hips and surveyed the chaotic scene. He barked orders, and his soldiers lined up along the fallen bus.

"Take over, Captain," he ordered and stomped away toward Carter. "I want to see that bus driver when you're done."

The captain positioned the men, some with ropes, and explained what he wanted done, and then as everyone else watched and commented, the soldiers pushed and pulled the bus upright.

The passengers cheered. The driver clapped the closest three soldiers on the back, jumped into the bus, swung his arms, and yelled at the passengers to get in.

The captain went to the driver's window, and the driver got out and stomped over to the general.

"Great good work!" the driver said, beaming. "Thank you very much!"

The general nodded curtly, understanding the Arabic.

"You see a caravan like us?" The general pointed in the direction from which the bus-truck had come, the direction toward which the American caravan was going—northwest.

"You bet! Going hell-fast!"

"How far?"

"Day," the Arab driver said, "maybe day and a half."

"All right," the general said, pursing his lips. He waited until the Arab understood that he was dismissed, then the general said in English, "Scum."

"Then why help them, General?" Elena asked.

"Good PR." The general crossed his arms.

"What he's saying is that it's in America's economic and military interests to keep the Arabs happy," Carter said.

The driver was back in the bus, turning on the motor.

"Chevron! Chevron! Chevron!" a passenger shouted out the window to the soldiers in thanks, thinking that the American soldiers were Chevron oil workers.

"We want to be as rich as Saudi Arabia!" shouted another passenger, laughing.

"More oil! More money! More wives!" yelled a third.

The bus-truck's motor wasn't turning over. The driver tried again, and this time there was coughing and sputtering. Encouraged, the driver banged his palm on the steering wheel and turned the ignition once more as the good-natured passengers settled into their seats. For ten minutes he sweated and tried to start the vehicle. He kept up a running conversation with the passengers, and whenever one offered advice he stopped to listen. Finally he threw up his hands and stalked back out onto the sand. He opened the motor compartment and gazed inside.

"*Malesh*," a toothless old Arab said to the driver as he followed the driver outside. "Never mind." The old Arab put a mat on the sand in the shade of the bus-truck, sat down, took out an apple, and ate and watched the driver probe the motor.

The two soldiers had finished their tour of the under-parts of the jeeps and trucks and were reporting to their sergeant.

"*Inshallah, bukra!*" the bus driver announced to the waiting passengers, his face resigned. "God willing, tomorrow it will be fixed!"

"Time to go, sir," a soldier said to Carter.

Elena's guard helped her into her jeep, his hand protectively on her elbow. She stared stoically at Carter, then dropped her eyes.

Carter walked back to his jeep, drank deeply from his canteen, and got in. Was there someone in the camp besides Elena Markova and Phillips who would have killed the radioman? Was there someone else who wanted to radio out?

The bus passengers had set up a colorful camp in the shade of the bus-truck. The driver was spreading the gearbox's pieces out on a blanket, checking each minutely, occasionally scratching his head before he went on to the next piece.

"Think he knows what he's doing?" Carter's driver asked him.

"Probably the only one who does," Carter said. "That's not an assembly-line motor. It's been tinkered together, and the way the driver's working on it, he may have built it himself."

The general stood up and waved the caravan into motion. They left behind the bus-truck and its passengers in their isolated camp, who were now telling stories and jokes and sharing a bottle of "Khartoum sherry," a date wine. Centuries before, the Arabs had quit worrying about the desert. They accepted its hardships, planned for them, and refused to be stopped from their small pleasures.

Carter considered the human's ability to be resourceful.

"Did the radioman have any enemies?" Carter shouted to the driver as they lurched along.

"Nope! Good soldier! Followed orders!"

"Drug problems? Family problems? Money problems?"

The driver shook his head each time.

"General don't allow none!" the driver yelled back. *The general don't allow none.* A tough, reliable group of men, hand-picked, well trained, and loyal. The general might be vain, imperious, and arbitrary, but he knew how to select and train men who could do a job. Besides that, he loved his work, had the authority of the President of the United States, and the trust of the indomitable Hawk.

The caravan rode the rest of the afternoon without stopping, rode until the sky turned violet and saffron, and then, as they were making camp, Carter realized that there was something about one of the earlier nights in camp that was odd, that he should remember.

TWENTY-SIX

The Sudan is a large country, one third the size of the contiguous United States, and its vastness encompasses savannas, deserts, mountains, and the gigantic swamp, the Sudd. Besides its mixture of geography and Arabic north and black south, it is a mixture of old and new, the new struggling with the impractical visions and the throbbing urgency to grow from the old.

Outside the town of Wau in the southern Sudan is a new, vacant brewery that will probably never be used. The Sudan cannot afford to import hops and barley for the multimillion-dollar brewery to make beer. On the other hand, the Kenana Sugar Company—now one of the largest in the world—in northern Sudan is a success story. There, cane cutters earn four dollars a day—about three times the nation's per capita daily wage. Kuwait and Saudi Arabia have built a new sugar cane refinery there that has an annual capacity of more than 360,000 tons, and a modern city of fifty thousand has sprung up. The government is delighted and hopes to fulfill its slogan of becoming the "breadbasket of the Arab world" by continuing to successfully combine the Sudan's largely untouched resources with Western technology and Arab petrodollars.

Carter reflected on this the next morning as the caravan approached four Arab camel herders who had stopped to examine one of their camels' hooves. They stood in a circle and discussed the problem at length while the animal patiently waited for progress. Carter thought of the rickety Sudanese vehicles he'd seen over the past few days, of Sudan's primitive living conditions, of the Nilotes in their scars and traditional dress, of the Arabs in their long flowing djellabahs and turbans. Change that starts at the top often never reaches the bottom, but change that starts at the bottom always ferments up. When the ordinary citizens of the Sudan changed, the government would have to change—as would any government anywhere—and maybe not in the direction the leadership had planned.

The caravan passed the herders and camels, and Carter's trained ears suddenly registered a great mechanical roar over the usual noise of the caravan's travel.

Jets.

Impossible to hear earlier because of the jouncing racket on the track.

Carter shouted, pulled on the driver's shoulder, and pointed at the jets coming in low.

Three of them. Unmarked.

The driver leaned on the horn, and the jeep bounced out of control off the road.

The vehicles screeched to stops in clouds of sand. The travelers dived out.

Under the jeeps and trucks.

Bullets whining.

Strafing the sand and vehicles.

Someone screamed, hit.

A jeep's gas tank exploded.

Noise and dust as the jets passed over.

The soldiers scrambled out from under the vehicles, grabbed rifles, and manned the machine guns at the backs of the jeeps.

The machine gunners swiveled, following the jets as they circled around to make another pass over the caravan.

The general had his ivory-handled pistol in his left hand, his rifle in his right, as he stood angry and spraddle-legged in the center of the track, shouting defiance at the jets.

The jets roared back over the caravan, high, out of

range, their wings rocking as they shot northwest. The general fired his pistol after them.

"Come back and fight, you bastards!"

They watched the jets until they were only specks in the bright blue sky. At last the general dropped his pistol hand.

"Casualty report!" he yelled.

A medic ran toward the truck where someone had screamed. Other soldiers checked vehicles and supplies as black smoke from the burning jeep drifted over the caravan. The jeep was a total loss.

"Carter!"

Nick Carter walked over to the general.

"What do you think?" the general asked.

"Flogger-Es, the same kind of jet that came after me over the village."

"I know that!" The general was impatient. "Why'd they let us off so easy?"

"Warning, maybe."

"Maybe," the general echoed, his pale eyes appraising Carter. "Well, this does it." He swung an arm up onto Carter's shoulder. "Time for me to make the move. I got an assignment for you."

They walked away from the caravan, both still watching the vacant sky to the northwest.

"Been giving this some thought," the general said, then shouted over his shoulder. "I want this operation back on the road in ten minutes, Captain!"

The captain saluted smartly and trotted off to the burning jeep.

"What's the assignment, General?" Carter asked.

"Give me a minute, son," General Taylor said. "Never did have a boy of my own. Indulge me. Actually, never had any kid I knew about. Never got married, but that didn't keep me out of the sack!" He laughed heartily and withdrew the arm from Carter's shoulder to wipe his big white handkerchief across his sweating face. "Never had time for so-called normal life." He sighed. "Now, I've been watching you. I know what you think of me, my opinions. I heard all that smart-alecky stuff about Israelis and blacks and gooks of all kinds you were trying to shame me with. I don't mind. I've got just one standard—my country. All those others got their own countries, which is fine with me as long as they don't hurt my country. You know what I mean. Wars and oil and the 'accidental' shooting down of passenger planes. But I've had a problem lately. Don't seem to see eye-to-eye with the Pentagon these days. Some even want to retire me. Me! They think I'm an old, outdated warhorse, and maybe they're right. Course, I don't think so. They keep sending me on exploratory missions, then yanking me as soon as things settle down a little and they can send in their negotiators. I think they're nuts. They're so tolerant that they let other countries walk all over us.'' The general hit a fist into his palm. "It's got to stop! Right now! That's why I'm sending you back. I want you to tell them about the KGB agent murdering my radioman, about the jets, and about what happened down on the White Nile in that wiped-out village. I want those deskbound brass to see how bad it can get out here in the real world!''

"What if I said no, that Hawk has ordered me on this mission and I need to see it through?''

The general kicked sand and watched the grains settle back indistinguishable from the rest.

"It's my ball game now, Carter. Hate to pull rank, but there it is.''

Carter nodded.

"I'll take Markova with me,'' Carter said.

"She stays. Don't want you worrying about guarding someone. I want you to pay attention to your job, got that? Now there's a town called Muglad not far from here. Your driver'll have a map. You take him and the jeep. There'll be telephones in Muglad. Nearest airport's north, in al-Bashir, I think. Anyway, once you get to a phone, should take you only a few hours to get back to Washington. Then you can report to Hawk and get over to the Pentagon, too. Got that?''

"I understand the orders,'' Carter said.

"You don't sound too happy, boy. But that's life." The general slapped Carter on the shoulder. "You know the great United States of America hasn't won a war in thirty years? Now *that's* something to *really* be unhappy about!"

Carter and the driver retraced the caravan's journey over the track. The endless track and flat, arid land had been unrelentingly the same for so long—and would continue that way for the general and his caravan until they reached Nyala—that, if it weren't for the sun, Carter wouldn't know which direction he and the driver were going. They rode in silence past the occasional scrub bushes and trees of the desert landscape, past ibex and desert antelope bounding gracefully away, and past a gaggle of skinny-legged ostriches who ran as if their feet were too big for them.

They rode without stopping to rest, faster than the caravan had, the driver confident of the jeep, and he and Carter eager to finish the bone-rattling journey. They were heading back to a track that branched off north to Muglad. They would follow it for several more hours until they got to the desert city.

But when they reached the intersection, Carter pulled out Wilhelmina.

"We'll stay on the east track," Carter said, the Luger pointed at the soldier's chest.

The soldier glanced at the gun, thin-lipped, angry.

The driver yanked the steering wheel to the right.

Off the track, into the soft sand.

And lunged for the Luger.

Carter slammed an elbow into the soldier's jaw, almost knocking him over the top of the jeep door.

The motor stalled, stopped.

The soldier's head lolled, his eyes closed.

Unconscious.

Carter dragged the soldier across the seat, tied his hands and feet, and anchored him to the jeep seat. Then he refilled the jeep's tanks, checked the tires, and drove back onto the track.

Heading east. Even faster.

The hot, dusty miles ate up the morning, then the early afternoon. Carter hoped that he would be in time. The soldier woke up, complained, and Carter knocked him out again. Carter wanted the companionship of only his own thoughts. He had a lot of figuring to do, and, if he was right, he had some planning to do as well.

The bus-truck from the day before was still beside the road, the driver-mechanic bustling his passengers into the cagelike bus. They waved and called when they saw Carter.

"Chevron is back! Chevron! Oil! Saudi Arabia!"

Carter talked to the passengers and found what he wanted: an American-made digital watch. Carter bought the watch on the spot with American dollars. The Arab face of the former owner was radiant as he licked his thumb to count the bills.

"I have another fare for you," Carter told the bus driver.

The driver was sitting behind the steering wheel on a seat fashioned from a molded plastic kitchen chair. The base was wired to a piece of wood that was nailed into the bus's plywood floor.

"Not much room," the driver said, turning around to face the confusion and advice from the passengers who nearly filled the bus.

"He needs two seats so he can sleep." Carter got out his billfold. "Too much beer," Carter said, twirling a finger around his ear. "Made him crazy, so I had to tie him up."

Carter counted out bills until the driver held up a hand, embarrassed.

"Too much," the driver said, handing back one bill.

Carter knew he had still paid four times the ordinary fare from Nyala to Malakal.

The driver put the bills into his robe.

"Rich American, poor Sudanese," he explained and grinned.

Carter shook his hand and went for the soldier.

He stretched the soldier on a double seat under a window facing north. An old woman in a *tobe* made from a single piece of cloth leaned over the young man.

"Very pretty," she observed.

"Sit down, old woman!" shouted an Arab.

"You going all the way to Malakal?" Carter asked her.

"I am! I am!" cried a middle-aged man, his hand held out.

"What about you?" Carter asked the woman.

She patted the soldier's cheek.

"I'll take him with me," she said. "No charge."

Carter handed her money so she wouldn't take it out in trade.

"Know where the airport is there?" he said.

She dropped the money down her front, wiggled.

"Is it important?" she asked.

The bus driver stomped down the aisle, shoving passengers aside.

"Pig!" complained one to the driver.

"Dictator!" said another.

"Don't worry, Chevron!" the bus driver said. "I am a bus company employee! I will see he gets there. Part of the service!"

He took Carter's arm and led him up the aisle.

"You see, I am used to responsibility," the bus driver explained as he opened the door for Carter. "The reputation of my country is in these hands." He spread them for Carter to see. "Besides, you have already paid me! Bye-bye!"

Carter grinned and walked to his jeep. The bus driver had put floorboards under the wheels that had spun into the sand. The bus was completely reloaded, the chickens and goats back on the roof, the passengers in their seats.

The bus driver sat down again, rubbed his hands, and turned on the ignition.

The passengers were silent.

Waiting.

The motor sputtered, caught, and roared into life.

Everyone cheered. It had been a community effort.

The old woman leaned out the window.

"The pretty one will get there safe!" She smacked her wrinkled lips. "Such good care he'll get!"

Carter laughed and waved.

The bus inched forward, its wheels catching the boards on the sand.

The bus climbed out of its hole, and the driver slowly angled it toward the track. Once there and reluctant to leave the wheel, he ordered three men out to retrieve the floorboards. They dashed out, picked up the pieces, threw them on the roof next to the animals, and hopped back into the bus.

The bus drove away, brown arms waving out the windows, heads craning for a last look.

Carter waved in return, then he took out the radio that looked like a tape cassette. He pried apart the digital watch. He pressed the watch's battery into the recess of a nickel-sized piece of metal he'd taken from the radio. There was a tiny seam that rimmed the metal piece's edge that, when pried open, would show the insides of a powerful homing device that worked in conjunction with satellite electronics. It was an engineering feat that would have been considered a miracle ten years before. Carter put the "nickel" back inside the fake recorder's case. There was one remaining "nickel" left there, too. When the time came, he could enter the coordinates onto the recorder's keyboard and they would be locked into the battery-powered "nickel," giving Hawk his exact location.

Carter stuffed the fake recorder into his backpack, turned on the jeep's ignition, and drove off at breakneck speed down the track after General Taylor's caravan. Tomorrow the caravan would catch up with the rebel Sudanese soldiers and their American advisers.

TWENTY-SEVEN

It was dawn when Nick Carter saw them, a blue-gray dawn with a broadening band of pink on the horizon behind him and a vast steel-gray blade on the horizon before him. The caravan was already moving on the track, the vehicles' dust misleadingly pale and weak-looking. There was no sign yet of the Sudanese forces.

Carter slowed and fell back, content to wait for the inevitable meeting. Then he would figure the coordinates and lock them into the homing device because, if his calculations were correct, there was no way that Taylor would be the only victor.

Carter followed the caravan at enough distance that the trucks and jeeps looked like toys wobbling with the play of an unruly child. He thought about Elena Markova. She would be all right for a while still.

The sun rose, and heat shimmered and danced above the land. Black-robed nomads riding camels passed in a string, ignoring the caravan and then Carter. A secretary bird stood unmoving on the top branch of a solitary thorn tree, caught in a black silhouette by the sunlight as if it were the living insignia of the Sudan that it had become. The previous symbol—the white rhino—had grown too scarce.

Carter followed the caravan for two hours, noting that General Taylor was not ordering his usual rest stops for the vehicles and men. Also that he was traveling faster, like a desert stallion sniffing water.

The plain stretched endlessly, part of the broad savanna

belt that begins at the southern edge of the Sahara Desert and extends across the African continent. The land varied somewhat. It was either flat or rolled monotonously. Occasionally there were the sand dunes born thousands of years ago and now partially or completely fixed by dry vegetation. But here, along the track, the land was sandy and flat, with the usual assortment of desert birds, skeletal remains of animals and vehicles, and, once, Carter saw far off a pride of lions gold against the sky.

He spotted the clouds of sand first.

Enormous clouds on the far side of Taylor's caravan. Circling now.

Out onto the desertlike savanna.

Around.

Then he saw that they were a caravan of trucks and jeeps, like Taylor's. Circling Taylor's.

No gunfire.

Taylor's caravan moved off the track onto the savanna.

Circling, too, like two dogs sniffing the same bone.

Not a single shot.

Carter stopped the jeep and grabbed his backpack. He needed to figure the coordinates.

Phillips laughed at Elena Markova. *KGB bitch*, he thought.

"Attack!" Elena yelled, pounding her bound fists on the jeep's dashboard. "Attack!"

The jeeps' and trucks' motors were off, and General Taylor got out of his jeep with the two American flags. He crossed his arms and waited, ignoring Elena.

There was no way the general was going to attack. He was confirming Phillips's view of life that everyone is out for himself. Survival of the fittest, and the fittest survive in style.

Colonel al-Barzani in his spit-and-polish uniform strode across the savanna to meet the general. Beside al-Barzani was Prince Mujahid in his kaffiyeh and robes, sparkling white in the heat. The two men walked like a team.

The three leaders met and then moved off together, talking at the same time, to consult alone in the savanna.

A helicopter flew overhead heading east. It had no markings.

Carter worked fast, his trained fingers nimble, but he wasn't fast enough. The helicopter's blades sent sand billowing like mushroom clouds. Its roar filled Carter's head.

No time.

He flicked the jeep on and raced back along the track.

Gunfire.

Shots spitting into the sand and jeep.

Carter careened off the track and grabbed Wilhelmina.

A black face from the helicopter overhead laughed arrogantly down.

Carter shot.

The face screamed and exploded.

The body in the Sudanese uniform fell out, the arms and legs moving as if alive.

The sudden loss of weight made the helicopter jerk, then the unseen pilot righted the machine and flew on.

Carter wrenched the steering wheel hard right, heading directly away from the caravans and into the wilderness of the savanna.

The helicopter rushed back toward Carter.

Carter drove hard left, then hard right, zigzagging abruptly.

The helicopter tried to follow.

The pilot's reflexes were not as quick and the machine not as flexible.

Still, the pilot peppered the jeep with more bullets.

Carter drove on, but he knew it was hopeless.

Inevitably he would be killed. There was nowhere to escape in the flat, shelterless land. The helicopter had the advantages of height and range. Carter was beneath and exposed. Carter hadn't even had time to fix the coordinates for Hawk's homing device. His only chance was to kill the helicopter pilot.

As the pilot passed over again, Carter drove with one hand and shot into the helicopter's belly.

If the pilot would only lean out. . . .

The helicopter whirred away, the sound of the machine like humiliating laughter.

Carter drove on, over the blistering savanna.

Then he heard the helicopter coming up behind.

He did a quick U-turn.

It was only a moment, but he saw the pilot's eyes.

And shot.

Between the eyes.

Carter smiled.

Then he saw the machine coming down.

Too late to run.

Pulled the ''nickel'' out, turned it on.

Popped it in his mouth.

Swallowed.

At least that much done as the helicopter fell like a broken bird onto Nick Carter's jeep.

The caravans' troops stopped their work to watch the battle between the jeep and the helicopter. They gawked like a bunch of tourists. Phillips shook his head in disgust.

''Carter,'' one of the soldiers told another.

Phillips walked away, looking for the radio, as the helicopter dropped dead on the jeep.

Al-Barzani shouted orders, and a jeep peeled off into the desert. The soldiers continued to watch. Elena Markova's sick face made Phillips smile.

The radioman was drinking from his canteen.

''Got any coffee?'' Phillips inquired.

''Now?'' the radioman said. His fair hair was almost white against his pink, sunburned face. The radio was beside him.

''Why not? We're going to be here a while.''

The radioman shook his head.

''Not my department.'' He drank more water, then turned to gaze at al-Barzani's jeep as it approached the crash.

Phillips waited, watching with the radioman. *Egypt would want the information for sure. And they'll pay.* The Sudan and Egypt shared a long border, and Egypt was just a short hop across the Red Sea to Saudi Arabia. *Egypt would pay good,* he thought. Now that Phillips saw what was going on, he could scare the hell out of them and they'd pay maybe enough at last for him to retire. He was ready to retire. This operation had taken a lot out of him. He felt paper-thin, even to himself. It was the heat and being at the general's mercy. He liked to work alone. Didn't like to take orders. Didn't like someone else to have the gun. He touched his empty holsters.

"General wants to see you," a soldier said, running up to the radioman.

Phillips came alert.

"On my way," the radioman said and screwed the lid onto his canteen.

The two soldiers glanced at the jeep that was now driving pell-mell back across the desert to rejoin the caravans, then the radioman and the messenger raced off to the cluster of three leaders who were also watching the jeep.

Phillips glanced around. He'd like to take that nurse with him. She was a wildcat with her sharp fingers and flower-smelling hair. Maybe he'd go back for her, really go back. They'd live in France where her skin would be appreciated, and every night they'd have a war in bed. He'd win, as he had in the Dinka village, her terrified eyes and hoarse voice begging for death with her tribe, or at least death.

The soldiers around Phillips were occupied watching the desert. Soon they'd go back to their tasks. He sat down at the radio. He didn't need much time. He was a professional.

Nick Carter awoke in the jeep as the desert exploded with the thunder and shaking of the helicopter and jeep's gas tanks. The soldier next to him turned back around, his M-1 held upright.

"Nice shot!" his companion shouted in Arabic from the front seat.

The soldier nodded modestly. On his sleeve was the patch of the Zab Brigade, and Carter smiled grimly. Al-Barzani's men. He wasn't surprised.

At least he'd had time to swallow the homing device. It wouldn't bleep out the coordinates, but it would still bleep. It would take longer, but Hawk could home in on it. And no search of Carter would ever reveal it. He should be able to keep it in his system for at least twenty-four hours, and then it would stay in a latrine, still working, until the battery gave out.

"He's awake!" the soldier with the rifle shouted into the front seat as the jeep spun into the caravan.

Phillips worked across the radio's band, looking for the right wavelength. If he remembered correctly, it would be. . . .

The first bullet cut Phillips's spinal cord.

Phillips flopped like a salamander onto the sand, feeling nothing.

He screamed. His legs wouldn't move.

General Taylor laughed.

Al-Barzani and Prince Mujahid guffawed.

Phillips stared at them, tears overflowing his eyes. He wanted to feel it. He wanted to feel the pain.

"Your turn," the prince said in Arabic.

"Where do you want it?" al-Barzani asked. "You are our warning, and it's only fair that you choose."

Phillips looked at their pistols.

"I can't feel it!" he cried.

The general handed Phillips's Python revolvers to al-Barzani.

"Perhaps this will help."

"No! They're mine!"

Al-Barzani emptied the guns into Phillips, slowly, and Phillips sank back, bleeding into the sand, dying, as in his mind he was again a child running down the long brick street in Montreal, aching with the familiar pain and humiliation of Monsieur Robaire.

TWENTY-EIGHT

The modern prefabricated buildings rose like cereal boxes on the savanna's sands. Nick Carter figured they were somewhere outside Nyala, far enough away that only an occasional nomadic wanderer would see the strange buildings and wonder, perhaps relating on his travels that yet another miracle had happened in Allah's land.

There were six buildings the size of warehouses, and around them was unrolled barbed wire guarded by soldiers in jeeps. To the left, parked beyond the barbed wire, a cluster of Flogger-Es faced a long flat strip of land with the tire marks of a runway. More soldiers patrolled there. Carter saw American soldiers, Iraqis, Sudanese, Saudis, and Libyans from Colonel Kaddafi's Islamic Legion. At last, definite proof of a Kaddafi connection. Carter noted that there were many Libyan officers.

As the long caravan drove into the complex of buildings, a white man in a light blue leisure suit stood on the steps of the central building in the late afternoon sun. Carter watched him from the distance until at last he could make out the face.

Melvin J. Cooley, Universal Mining & Refining.

The jeeps carrying General Taylor, Colonel al-Barzani, and Prince Mujahid drove up to Cooley. The leaders got out, and all four men talked. Then they walked into the building that appeared to be the headquarters.

Carter watched their movements. Watched for signs of one giving orders to the others. But just as all three had

seemed equals on the savanna, here at the headquarters all
four seemed equal. Who was the leader of these commanders? Was it the so-called Mahdi?

"Okay, Killmaster," the guard who sat beside Carter
said. "Let's go. Too bad you didn't get away when you
had the chance."

The soldier walked Carter at gunpoint to the headquarters while around them the other soldiers unloaded jeeps
and trucks, looked on a bulletin board for sleeping assignments, and memorized the map that told the name and
use of each building.

From the back of the caravan, Carter at last saw Elena.
Her face was sunburned and angry, her eyes flashing like
knives.

"This is a fine mess!" she muttered as she joined him
on the doorstep.

"Still have a question about where my loyalties lie?"

"Neither mine nor yours," she said firmly. "This is
outrageous! They could start a nuclear war that would kill
us all!"

"Maybe that's what they have in mind," Carter said as
they stepped inside.

The four men were seated around a long table. Air
conditioning units hummed faintly in the distance. The
room was cold and stale, and the men who watched them
were colder, with human qualities about on a par with the
air conditioners.

"Well, Carter," General Taylor said, "you are a fool.
If you'd done what you were told, you'd remain alive."

"And you'd have taken the first step toward vindica-
tion," Carter said. "You were in Baghdad for the coup,
weren't you, General?"

"Killmasters are alleged to have something on the
ball," the general observed, smiling.

"In the room at al-Gaillani's palace with Cooley and
the colonel," Carter finished.

"He knew!" Cooley said. "Well, well! How'd you
like a job in my organization? I could use some smarts
instead of all the educated ninnies Harvard sends me."

"Appreciate your talent," Elena told him. "You won't find all that much among the amoral."

"Kill them!" Prince Mujahid said, his eyes burning. "Heathens! They'll never help the cause!"

"Not yet," cautioned General Taylor.

"They know a lot, especially about their respective espionage organizations," Cooley said thoughtfully.

"Perhaps they can be convinced," al-Barzani said, laying a dagger on the table.

"I thought you were doing fine without us, Cooley," Carter said. "You managed to get General Taylor assigned to 'rescue' me."

"Wasn't all that hard, really," Cooley said, rubbing his thumb and index finger together. His skin was white, the color of a hard-boiled egg, completely untouched by the sun even in the Middle East. "My company gets around."

"You mean your company has debts that can never be paid off," Elena said. "Capitalists!"

"All countries have debts like that," the general said. "Russia's bureaucracy is the worst abuser of all. This time we worked the system *for* us!"

"Just a suggestion whispered in the correct ear," Cooley said, grinning at his power. "Besides, the general and I are old buddies, you know? He's gonna work for us when he retires, right, T.S.?"

The general nodded.

Elena watched, her fists tight at her sides.

"First the suggestion," she said, "then a threat that sounds like a gentle reminder of what's owed."

"Now, now," the general said genially, "we're here to make friends, not stir up old animosities. We're doing something important here . . . . combine all these two-bit warring countries into one big Islamic nation. Look at the oil and potential natural resources that're being squandered. It's to all our advantages to help. Isn't that right, gentlemen?"

"How're you going to pull it off?" Carter asked. "You've got stalemates in two countries and an army based in a remote area. Doesn't sound like a winning plan to me."

"Believe me!" The prince pounded the table. "We'll win!"

"We have a way," the general said quietly.

For a moment there was silence, a heavy silence that convinced Carter that the men had a plan big enough to do just what they threatened. He looked at the certainty in their faces.

"Are you with us?" al-Barzani said, fingering his dagger.

"We'll need to think about it," Carter said. "Elena?"

"A few days," she said.

"Tomorrow," the Saudi prince said, his swarthy face twisted with his hunger for power.

"Tomorrow!" the others echoed.

TWENTY-NINE

Nick Carter and Elena Markova were imprisoned in a windowless room at the end of one of the warehouse-type buildings. There was no furniture, and the walls were reinforced with steel. The cold, air-conditioned air dried their sweat into the dust that covered them. The soldiers had long ago stripped away their belongings, including all that their pockets held.

"I missed you," Elena said teasingly.

"Not as much as I missed you," Carter said, grinning, "especially when I had that chopper on my tail."

She took his hand.

"Now what do we do?" she asked.

"I could use a shower to start, then a few tools of the trade."

Elena laughed.

"I don't think you'll get either here," she said. "Constant frustrations. Even Phillips. Damn him. I didn't get to kill him. Al-Barzani did. It was more like an execution."

There was a sound at the door.

Carter nodded to Elena and jumped up.

A key turned in the lock.

Carter ducked behind the door, and Elena smoothed her filthy camouflage trousers.

The door handle moved.

"Food!" a voice yelled out in Arabic as the door slowly opened, Carter still behind it.

Two Arabs in the full black burnooses and veils of the Tuareg came in. One carried two trays, and the other carried an M-1. Through the crack in the door, Carter saw a guard pass down the hall.

"Please put it on the table," Elena said brightly in Arabic. "And light the candles. A little dinner music would be nice, too. Help my appetite."

As Carter lunged out, the Arab with the M-1 swung the rifle into the other Arab's head and kicked the door closed.

The Arab fell soundlessly to the concrete floor.

Elena dove for the trays.

"Now what?" she exclaimed from the floor, balancing the trays precariously.

"Pretty kettle of fish you've gotten yourself into, Killmaster," the veiled guard said in Arabic. "Nice to see you again, Elena."

Carter and Elena stared at the robed figure.

"What a jaunt!" the voice went on in very British English. "Hold this, will you?" He handed the M-1 to Carter and took off his headdress.

Carter stared dumbfounded at the beaming face of Cecil Young.

"Have any of those fine burners left, Nicky? I certainly would enjoy one right now."

"Cecil!"

Carter leaned the M-1 against Elena and clapped both hands on the old man's shoulders.

"We thought you'd died!"

"Not that I know of, Nicky. But it was a scrape. Let's see what these hooligans are feeding us for dinner."

They uncovered the food.

Elena whistled.

"Sorry," she said. "An American habit I picked up somewhere."

The trays contained thick slices of rare prime rib, Yorkshire pudding, sliced beets, roasted carrots, and salads of butter lettuce, green onions, and fat tomatoes.

"This might even be enough to fill me up," Carter mused.

"Just remember that there are three of us, lad," Cecil Young said and sat cross-legged on the floor. "To what great good fortune do we owe this feast?''

"They're trying to buy us," Elena said as she busily divided the food. "It's a good way to go. I was beginning to think I'd die wrapped up in a tin like C rations."

They ate ravenously, the food better than any they remembered, and much more satisfying than their savanna daydreams.

At last they sat back, satiated, smiling weakly.

"Oh, God," Elena sighed.

"Yes, indeed," Young murmured.

"Could you get us more?" Carter asked.

Elena slapped Carter's flat stomach.

"Enough! Even for you, Nick!"

"She likes me again, Cecil," Carter said.

"It's very impudent for children to fight," Young said. He stretched out on the floor, raised his knees, and crossed them. "Oh, for a good burner!"

Carter got up and went at last to the sprawled Arab.

"Dead," Carter said, his fingers on the Arab's throat. "No pulse." He sat back on his heels. "I suspected Taylor from the beginning," he explained, "but wasn't sure right away. He heard us in the village because he was on the exact wavelength that Phillips was radioing out on—and that was the wavelength of the attacking force. It could have been sheer luck that Taylor found that wavelength, but more likely he knew it already. And the only way he'd know was to be in on the attackers' game."

"Sound reasoning, my boy," Young said. "Fill me in on everything that's happened."

Carter sat beside Elena and they related the story.

"I can see why you were suspicious of each other," Young said, "but obviously Nicky must have decided somewhere along the line that Taylor wasn't to be trusted, and that you were, Elena."

"It was the coincidence of the broken radios," Carter said. "At first I accepted that mine could have quit on its own, but then the general said that Elena's was broken, too. When she told me hers had gone out the same night mine had, I figured Phillips must have done it, although I could see no logical reason. Then, later, I remembered that Phillips spent that first night tied up. He couldn't have done it since it was only the next morning that the general released him. Then I was left again thinking it was the general. He seemed to be the only one who might have something to gain. But what? It became more apparent when I remembered that he'd made up to Elena, then discredited her by blaming her for the radioman's death. He probably killed the radioman in as barbaric a way as possible because that's his vision of how Russians operate. And it gave him the excuse he needed to send me back to Washington to plead his case while he kept Elena around until he had time to question her with his coup friends.''

"So you came back," Elena said. "And now you're stuck here too."

"What about you, Cecil?"

Young closed his eyes and cleared his throat.

"It's this way, children," he said. "There was a bloody awful coup in Riyadh. A dreadful mess, but in the end a stalemate. Since I speak Tuareg—Berber, too," he added, enjoying his lack of modesty, "I managed to drop out of sight long enough to get into costume and join Mujahid's murdering crew. It seems the ultrafanatic Muslims are bent on taking over their countries and the whole Arab world. That's general information now, I suppose, but they want to destroy Israel . . ."

"Taylor won't mind that," Elena commented.

"A burr under his breeches, no doubt," Young said. "Anyway, the leaders knew the coups would be either very messy or standoffs because of the deeply entrenched governments they were taking on, so they arranged a little trump card to get everyone to give up. . . . Or, if that didn't work, they'd simply use it." Young wiped a hand over his mustache, then tugged on the ends. "Did I tell you that they're all a bunch of rotters?"

"You did give that impression, yes," Carter said and smiled.

"Oh, well. There it is. The trump is to proclaim Kaddafi the Mahdi because Libya's part in this has been to build a prototype American B-1 bomber from plans of Taylor's.''

Young paused for effect, obviously enjoying the complete attention of Elena and Carter. He pulled on his mustache again.

"Then they'll load it," Young said, "with two atomic bombs stolen from American bases by Melvin Cooley's men.''

"Impossible!'' Elena said. "Even America's security isn't that bad!''

"Highly unlikely,'' Carter agreed. "Are you sure of your information, Cecil?''

Cecil Young nodded soberly.

"No one knows the bombs are gone yet,'' he explained. "The soldiers who took them are on Cooley's private payroll. They substituted fake bombs for the real ones. Take a long time to ferret out.''

Carter and Elena stared at one another.

"Just what you'd said,'' Elena murmured, astounded.

"The ultimate threat,'' Carter said. "And death for them is just a fast way to their God.''

"Of course,'' Young said, still deep in his story, "Universal Mining and Refining will stay strong and profitable and in the good graces of the winners, whoever they are.'' He sighed. "They are a group of lovely men.''

"But who will they bomb?'' Elena wanted to know. "Certainly not themselves . . .''

"Israel!'' Young said, sitting up. "Israel! They figure that'll put them on the Arab's team, and if it doesn't, it'll at least scare them out of their pants and into line!''

They stared at one another.

"They won't back off now,'' Elena said.

"Can't,'' Carter added.

"Well,'' Cecil Young said, rubbing his hands, "now for *our* plans!''

Carter stretched.

"Did I mention the homing device?'' he asked innocently.

"You have one?" Elena said, jumping up. "Where? They took everything."

"Not everything. I swallowed it."

Cecil Young slapped Carter on the back.

"Good for you, lad! That's resourcefulness! Unfortunately, we do have a problem connected with that."

"I'm afraid to ask," Carter said.

"Tight security here," the elderly gentleman said, dragging on his bushy mustache. "All communication out is electronically jammed."

"Damn!"

"But we do have me, don't we?" Young smoothed his robes and grinned like a pixie. "Gad! It's good to be out of retirement and back in the trenches!"

Carter and Elena laughed.

Cecil Young described the Day of the Mahdi complex, the security measures, and the soldiers' routines.

"Drills all day long," he said. "Those commanders know how to work their men. Keeps them in line, you know. No women and no spirits, so you've got to work them."

"Have you heard any rumblings?" Carter asked. "Any of the soldiers unhappy with the ethics of the operation?"

"Nary a twitter," Young said. "The Arabs believe it's a matter of religion, and the Americans are following their beloved leader. For all of them, it's a matter of loyalty and trust."

"What's the sequence of events?" Carter asked.

Cecil Young's face fell.

"I was afraid you'd ask that, lad. It's a bit of a sticky wicket. Not much time."

"Time for what?" Elena asked.

"To save Israel," Young answered, his eyes full of worry. "The warnings went out today. The first bomb drops tomorrow. Noon. On Israel. The plane takes off from here at eleven o'clock, Kaddafi is declared the Mahdi, and the renegade troops throughout the Middle East will be whipped into a frenzy to win the coups."

"And the second bomb?" Carter's voice was like ice.

"Not specified yet. Probably destined for Egypt. No one loves Egypt since Anwar Sadat made peace with Israel."

The three sat, looking at one another until at last Cecil Young shrugged, helpless.

"Sorry, children. I tried to get out to send a message of the base's location and that the bombs would be coming from here."

The old agent hung his head, miserable.

Carter smashed a fist into his palm.

"Who's in charge here?" he said.

"No one and everyone," Young said slowly. "A Roman triumverate: General Taylor because he's Cooley's man and Cooley has got the bombs, Colonel al-Barzani because he's the ranking Islamic military man, and Prince Mujahid representing Islamic royalty. Kaddafi, of course, is scheduled to be the religious leader, but no one really trusts him to stay long in that spot. Basically, Taylor and al-Barzani are calling most of the plays because they're the military men."

"We've got to knock the operation out here!" Carter said.

"Looks like the only way," Elena agreed.

"I like the way you talk," Cecil Young said. "Have any ideas?"

The three sat silently and considered.

"There's no way and no time to win them over," Cecil Young muttered.

"And there are only three of us anyway," Elena added.

"Three is all it'll take," Carter said. *"They're* outnumbered. Cecil, can you get my radio?"

"Give me a few hours, Nicky."

"Okay. Then this is what we'll do . . ."

THIRTY

The night passed slowly. Nick Carter and Elena Markova slept with their arms wrapped around one another as if they were the last people in the world. They awoke to the sounds of jeeps backfiring, the babble of many languages, and the booted feet of soldiers walking up and down the corridor outside their prison room.

Despite his bravado of a few hours earlier, Carter was deeply worried. Several thousand well-trained soldiers were in the complex, protected by advanced security measures and alert commanders whose orders monitored airwaves, skies, and events in countries across the world.

Carter, Elena, and Cecil Young would have to be quick when the time came—and lucky—to succeed at their desperate plan. Too much of it depended on Carter's assessment of the personalities of the leaders and on his knowledge of how to use peoples' weaknesses against themselves. It was chancy all the way down the line.

"Have you ever been to Leningrad?" Elena asked, turning in his arms.

"Not for years. Why?" He stroked her hair.

"It's never forgotten World War Two," she said softly. "Hitler killed more than a million people there. Mostly starvation from the siege, but bombing, too. Now when you walk down the streets you still see the shell marks on some of the buildings. The city has preserved them. And sometimes there are plaques, too."

"What do the plaques say?" Carter murmured in her ear, grateful for her diversion.

"They're warnings or memorials. One of them is funny. It says, 'Comrades!' "—she pounded her chest—" 'In case of shelling, this side of the street is the more dangerous.' "

Carter smiled.

"Russians."

"It's important to maintain a sense of humor," she said, curling around him. "It helps in the hard times."

As he kissed her, they heard the door open at last.

They sat up, and Cecil Young, covered from head to toe in his Tuareg disguise, sidled in aiming an M-1 at them. He was followed closely by al-Barzani and Prince Mujahid, their faces mottled with self-righteous rage. Last came a Sudanese medic who bent over the dead Arab in the corner of the room where Carter had dragged him.

"Dead!" the medic pronounced.

"I told you!" Cecil Young said in Tuareg dialect, playing his part. "I barely escaped! And when I told the American soldiers, they couldn't be bothered! We must have vengeance!"

"Dogs!" Prince Mujahid cried.

"Leni!" Al-Barzani looked balefully at her. His enormous chest was full of ribbons decorating his Zab Brigade uniform. "Mohammed will be disappointed. He's waiting for you in Baghdad."

Elena shrugged.

"The lieutenant's a pipsqueak," Elena said in English to Carter.

"What did she say?" the prince asked al-Barzani.

Al-Barzani translated anyway.

The prince bared his teeth and snarled.

"Whore!" he cried in Arabic.

Prince Mujahid had a long, handsome face, but the cheeks had the deep vertical creases that came from a life in the desert and too many hours spent in devout hatred.

"They must die!" the prince proclaimed. "Our soldiers must be honored!"

It was the verdict Carter wanted.

"Unfortunately," al-Barzani echoed in his modulated,

professional voice, "the prince is right. We can't have you going around killing our soldiers, especially when we offer you a hand in friendship. It will be the firing squad for you!"

A firing squad was not what Carter had in mind. He felt the weight of the morning hours heavily on him. He wished they had let him keep his wristwatch, and he dared not look at al-Barzani's or Prince Mujahid's.

"You call that friendship?" Carter said, pointing to the jeweled dagger in al-Barzani's belt.

"More like forced persuasion," Elena commented.

"Only the weak need more than words to win an argument," Carter observed.

Al-Barzani's face darkened, but his expression of benign disappointment remained. He needed to be pushed to anger.

"You deceived us, Leni," al-Barzani said, "first by pretending to be a German businesswoman who wanted to convert. Then you both deceived us by saying you'd consider our offer to join us." He spread his hands. "You see the ramifications. You're not to be trusted."

"Death to them and all like them!" Prince Mujahid shouted. "Death to my brother the king!" He spat on the concrete floor. "He calls himself a moderate, but I call him a weakling! I have the richest country in the world, the place of the sacred birth of Islam, and it's ruled by a *woman*!"

Carter smiled. The trick was to push the two men hard, but not so hard that al-Barzani and Mujahid would kill them on the spot. A matter of fine judgment.

"In that dress," Carter said to the prince, "you might as well be a woman."

The prince lunged forward, his robes spreading like a sheet, but al-Barzani, more self-controlled, grabbed his arm and held him.

"They're uneducated infidels," al-Barzani said soothingly. "Don't waste your energy on them."

"Ha!" Carter hooted. "Your oil doesn't buy brains or ethics!"

"Iraq is being abused," Elena added. "With idiots like you, Colonel."

"The Koran tries to make civilization from savagery. It's a losing battle," Carter said.

"A lost battle," Elena said. "We're looking at two losers, one in drag and the other in the unsoiled toy soldier clothes of a spoiled child."

"What are those ribbons for, Colonel? Bravery in carnival rides?" Carter said, pointing at the lavish display on the colonel's proud chest.

"Checkers?" Elena queried.

"Tiddledywinks!"

Carter and Elena looked at one another, then laughed in the now twitching, enraged face of al-Barzani.

"Enough!" al-Barzani shouted. "Out! Get them out of here!" He pushed the Tuareg at them.

"The desert?" Cecil Young suggested in Tuareg dialect as he ran around behind them, poking them up with the M-1. "It would be fitting!"

"The desert!" Prince Mujahid shouted, excited, smelling carrion.

"Infidels! Westerners!" al-Barzani raged.

"They must die in the desert!" the prince cried.

Cecil Young pushed Carter and Elena toward the door.

"You'll die slowly!" al-Barzani cried, outraged at the insult to himself and the righteous battles he had won. "Like the soulless animals you are!"

Carter and Elena walked down the long corridor, holding hands, quivering now and then, while behind them stalked Young with the M-1 and the two Arab leaders with their furious, self-righteous faces. Carter worried about what time it was. . . .

When they reached the blistering morning sun of the compound, al-Barzani stopped.

"Driver!" he yelled. "Driver!"

General Taylor was walking briskly across the compound toward them.

"Driver!" al-Barzani yelled again, beside himself. "I want a truck! Now!"

"What's going on?" General Taylor shouted. "What are you doing?"

A truck sped up to the doorstep, sand flying into their faces.

Al-Barzani ignored Taylor and went to the driver's window to give instructions, his hands waving. The prince stopped four soldiers with M-1 rifles who were coming off duty and told them to get into the truck. Other soldiers stopped to watch.

"I demand to know what's going on!" Taylor complained, drawing himself up to his full five-foot-nine.

"These . . . these . . ." Al-Barzani took several deep breaths. "They're going to be staked out in the desert! They killed a guard! They're never going to join us, and I refuse to put up with their profanities any longer! They disgrace us all!"

Melvin J. Cooley strode on his toothpick legs toward them.

"Gentlemen!" he exclaimed, his arms open, enclosing them all. "Gentlemen! Let's go inside and discuss this!"

Al-Barzani grabbed the prince's arm and dragged him back into the building.

"Bring them!" he told the Tuareg.

Cecil Young herded Carter and Elena back up the steps, and Cooley and General Taylor followed. Cooley took out a long, thin cigar, bit off the end, and stuck it between his teeth, frowning.

Al-Barzani kicked the door closed. Cooley lit his cigar and stared, his eyes mild but full of command, at the two Arabs and Taylor.

"I'd like an explanation," Cooley said. His voice had the authority of his two atomic bombs and the other services he could provide.

"They've got information we can use," General Taylor said, indicating Carter and Elena.

"They must die!" al-Barzani insisted. "We will accept nothing less. No compromises!"

"Vengeance!" the prince demanded.

Cooley considered the three leaders.

"I don't care how we get the information," General Taylor said, refusing to back down. "Let *them* question the agents, but we don't kill them. Not while I've got my men. You understand," speaking only to Cooley.

"This American general is just like my brother—always wants delays!" the prince fumed. "Cowards!"

General Taylor glared at Carter and Elena, then looked hard at the prince.

"I've had enough of you damned Arabs telling me what to do!"

He pulled his ivory-handled pistol from its holster and aimed it at the prince and al-Barzani. Instantly, the two Arabs produced long, curved daggers. They stepped forward.

"Seems to be only one way out," Cooley said quietly as he, too, drew a small pistol from his leisure jacket pocket and shot Brigadier General Thackery Simpson Taylor in the heart.

"Sorry, old buddy," he said. "You're expendable. The Arabs aren't."

The general fell to his knees, a hand over his chest, blood spreading around the fingers and across the immaculate uniform. The general's face was a mask of surprise and horror. He wouldn't die on a battlefield, and he was truly shamed. He closed his eyes and keeled over into his pooled blood on the concrete floor.

Cooley put the pistol back in his pocket and looked at the two Arab leaders.

"Better get him out of here."

The Arabs were grinning.

"Mine!" the prince announced and leaned over to pull General Taylor by the heels down the hall.

Cooley opened the front door and called out.

"Colonel Stevens!"

He held the door ajar until Colonel Stevens walked in, a sturdy man with thick features and shrewd eyes.

"Stevens," Cooley said, "I sent the general back to the States to command the operation from there." He closed the door. "You're in charge now. Don't screw up."

"Yes, *sir*!" Stevens saluted.

Al-Barzani gestured to Cecil Young in his Tuareg robes and Young hustled Elena and Carter once again out into the compound, now full of soldiers wondering what the excitement was all about.

Prince Mujahid joined Colonel al-Barzani on the doorstep while Cooley and Colonel Stevens watched attentively nearby.

The prince swung his robed arms into the air.

"Listen to me, brothers!" he shouted. "Come listen to me!"

The soldiers gathered around.

"We are here to fight a holy war!" Prince Mujahid said. "We have the strength of Allah and the knowledge of the Koran!"

More men gathered, the Arabs nodding, the Americans looking puzzled and watching Colonel Stevens for a clue as to what was happening.

"We must scourge the world of infidels! These two"—the prince pointed disdainfully at Carter and Elena—"have killed a brother! Struck him down before he could do Allah's work!"

Al-Barzani stepped forward.

"What must be done?" al-Barzani shouted. "What do you say?"

"Death!" the soldiers shouted in unison. "Death!"

"Is it the desert?" al-Barzani cried, his fist above his head.

"Yes! Yes!"

Cooley and Colonel Stevens, standing apart, nodded, giving the Americans the answer they wanted . . . everything was okay, the Arabs were just handling their own business.

Al-Barzani and the prince had proved their power. Al-Barzani dropped his fist, and the prince pushed Carter and Elena into the truck as the Arab soldiers in the compound cheered. Al-Barzani hooted, his hands on his hips, his head thrown back to the sun.

Then al-Barzani looked at the truck's driver.

"Take them away!" he ordered, staggering slightly, drunk with power.

Prince Mujahid jumped onto the back of the truck and waved, leering, as they drove off in a shower of sand.

THIRTY-ONE

Nick Carter, Elena Markova, Cecil Young with his Tuareg robes lumped around him, and the soldiers drove about two miles over the sandy savanna, drenched in sweat as the heat collected under the truck's tarpaulin. They were on no road or track, instead making their own trail across the wasteland. The soldiers were silent, their arms wrapped around their M-1s, their heads nodding with tiredness and the suffocating heat. Occasionally Prince Mujahid looked at Carter and Elena and chuckled to himself. Sweat rolled down his swarthy desert face unnoticed.

Abruptly the truck stopped, and the riders in back lurched.

Prince Mujahid leaped to the ground.

"Bring the ropes and stakes," he ordered.

Cecil Young pointed Carter and Elena off the truck and into the sand while a soldier opened a footlocker bolted into the truck bed. Inside were tools, ropes, and long stakes.

The prince danced away from the truck, excited. He looked at the flat land as if there would be one place particularly suited for painful death.

"Ahhh!" the prince sighed, staring pleased at a black vulture that circled over a scrub tree not far off. "Over here! Bring them over here!" He strode toward the tree. "It will be most convenient for our friend up there." He nodded at the gracefully flying scavenger. "With luck, he will go to work on you before you're dead!'' the prince said with a chuckle to Carter and Elena.

Cecil Young knocked the butt of his M-1 against Carter's and Elena's chests, and they fell back. The soldiers pulled the agents' arms and legs out, positioned the stakes, and pounded them deep so they would hold. Prince Mujahid handed down a roll of nylon rope.

''Would that it were leather!'' the prince said. ''Then I would wet the thongs so they would dry in the sun and stretch you like sheepskins!''

''Occasionally we get a break,'' Carter commented.

The soldiers tied Carter's and Elena's arms and legs tightly to the stakes, and the prince went around, testing the bonds.

''Nice work, yes?'' Elena inquired.

The prince glared at her.

''You won't think so soon,'' he said. ''Already the ropes are beginning to cut. The more you sweat, the more they will hurt. Salt and blood. By the time you repent, it will be too late.''

A broad smile spread across his crazed face as his limited imagination took over.

''Get in the truck,'' the prince ordered the soldiers. ''We must get back to witness our bomber's flight!''

The prince, the four soldiers, the driver, and Cecil Young strode back to the truck shimmering like a mirage in the late morning sun.

''The bomber must have arrived from Libya,'' Elena whispered to Carter.

''Probably came in at night,'' Carter said.

''It will get hotter!'' the prince called over his shoulder in farewell. ''And hotter and hotter! Until you wish to melt into the sands!''

''What about Cecil?'' Elena said. ''He's supposed to figure out a way to stay!''

''Be patient. Cecil's lived a long time because he knows what he's doing.''

The truck started, and a small doubt crept into Carter's mind. Suddenly there was a flurry of activity from behind the truck. Cecil Young jumped off, his Tuareg robes flying, and came running back to them. Prince Mujahid stared around the edge of the truck, watching.

Cecil pointed his rifle at the victims.

"I'm supposed to maim you to increase your suffering," he said as he shot into the sand next to Carter's leg. "Keep your eyes closed," he warned and shot next to Elena's arm.

The sand cut like needles into their flesh.

"You might scream, you know," Young said. "You're going to ruin my reputation."

Carter and Elena screamed as Young moved around them, shooting.

"Better go back to gunnery school," Elena said. "Your aim is terrible."

A shot seared Carter's wrist, drew blood, and cut his ropes.

"He also needs a bath," Carter said, then let out a scream. "I can smell him. Good shot, Cecil!"

Young bent as if to examine his work.

"Pay attention, children—I've got the coordinates," Young said as he stood above Carter's right hand and Elena's left. He gave them the coordinates, then added, "But I didn't know what size battery you needed, so I brought you a selection."

Suddenly a sand-colored bag fell softly to the ground from beneath Young's voluminous robes. It was inches from Carter's hand.

"Well, hi-ho and cheerio!" Young grinned, lifting his veil. "See you when we all pass over!"

"You're going back?" Elena asked.

"Must, dearie. Not to worry. Had a good run, eh?"

"Take care, Cecil," Carter said.

Cecil Young nodded and dashed away back to the truck.

"It's as you wished!" he shouted to the prince as he ran. "Their suffering will be of great magnificence!"

The truck did a sharp U-turn and returned down its path, fading into the brown savanna.

Carter and Elena grabbed at the bag with their bound hands.

"Dammit! He didn't cut the rope all the way!" Carter said, struggling against the nylon cord.

He pulled and twisted, drawing more blood on his wrist.

Elena worked with her fingernail, shredding the rope, until at last Carter was free.

He dumped open Young's bag.

"Watches!" Elena cried.

"Here's my radio," Carter said. "Can you read one and tell me what time it is?"

Elena arched her neck as Carter dropped the radio by his bound hand and rolled over to pick out the watch that would have the right size battery.

"Ten o'clock," she said.

"An hour. Hell!"

"Not much time," Elena agreed, her voice shaky.

Carter opened the watch, took out the battery, took the second and last "nickel" out of the tape recorder, put the battery in it, put the "nickel" back inside the recorder, then punched the coordinates onto the keyboard.

It was activated.

Carter fell back, and Elena sighed.

All they could do was wait.

And pray that Hawk had picked up Carter's signal while he was on the savanna the day before.

If Hawk had, he might be somewhere in the area, looking for Carter.

Carter sat up and began the slow work of setting himself and Elena free as the vulture swept over them.

When the ropes were at last untied, Elena and Carter shook their hands and legs to restore circulation.

"What time is it?" Elena asked.

"Ten-twenty now," Carter said.

They held hands silently, watching the vulture as it flew lower and lower. Its great black wings rode the air as if the currents were a bed, a comfortable bed for ease and sleep. The beaked face watched them as they watched it. Finally it landed ten feet off. It cocked its head, appraising its potential meal.

"Shoo!" Elena said, waving her hands. "Get out of here!"

Carter picked up a stone and threw it.

The bird hopped off, staring back sorrowfully. It stopped again to watch them.

The helicopter scared it off.

It flew up into the scrub tree to continue its hopeful vigil as the helicopter landed in a storm of wind and sand.

David Hawk stepped off in a business suit, a fat cigar jutting from his lips.

"Give me the story," he said. "Fast."

Carter told him about the complex and the two bombs waiting to be sent aloft in fifteen minutes.

Hawk stalked back to the helicopter and picked up a radiophone. He talked, the cigar still in his mouth, his lips working angrily around the familiar protrusion.

At last Hawk handed the radiophone back to the pilot.

"Dammit, N3," he said as he walked back to them, "you do wait until the last minute."

"Sorry, sir. What about the bomber?"

"First wave'll go in shortly. I'll take you in before the second. You'll have to get the bomber and those damned bombs out of there in between."

"Not much time," Elena said. "But we can do it."

Hawk stared at her.

"Elena Markova, I believe," he said formally and extended his hand.

"It's a pleasure, sir," she said. "Blenkochev speaks very highly of your work."

The handshake ended quickly, and the three ran to the helicopter. Hawk stuck his thumb up, and the helicopter took off. Carter glanced at the watch he'd adopted from the batch Cecil Young had left. It was 10:55.

A squadron of American jet bombers roared over them.

Dropped bombs onto the cereal-box compound.

The buildings exploded into fire and smoke.

Soldiers ran into the compound like ants scurrying

away from a fire storm.

The helicopter followed the bombers in. Soldiers on the ground fired at the low-flying helicopter. Hawk handed Elena and Carter new Lugers, and the helicopter hovered a few feet from the ground, close to the bombed-out Flogger-Es. The sophisticated Libyan-made B-1 bomber was straight ahead.

Prince Mujahid and Colonel al-Barzani raced across the tarmac, a squad of soldiers behind, heading toward the remarkable bomber. In the cockpit, the pilot leaned out the window, shouting for orders.

Carter and Elena jumped out of the helicopter, and it flew off. They crouched, aimed their Lugers, and fired.

Al-Barzani and the prince, intent on getting to the bomber, stumbled and rolled.

The prince struggled to get up and fell again into the arms of an attendant.

Al-Barzani crawled across the tarmac, shoving away the outstretched hands of his soldiers. Some of them turned and fired at Elena and Carter.

Elena and Carter dropped flat and fired back.

A shot rang out from the bomber.

Al-Barzani's head exploded and his soldiers screamed.

Carter and Elena dashed around the distraught men toward the bomber's closed door.

The Arab soldiers looked up.

Fired.

The door opened, and there was Cecil Young's unveiled face, grinning.

"Took you long enough, chappies," he said and leaped out, fixing his veil in place.

"Cecil!" Elena shouted after him.

"Good luck!" Carter yelled and locked the door.

They ran past the dead pilot, his throat slit tidily, and into the cockpit. More bombs were exploding in the compound as the second wave of American jets came in.

Elena stared at the advanced instruments.

"Good God!" she exclaimed. "Where do we start?"

Carter pointed and gave her quick instructions as bombs

flattened the buildings in the nearby compound. Debris struck their windows. Beneath them, Cecil Young, in his Tuareg robes, ducked. He was rallying the Arab soldiers to him, giving Carter and Elena much-needed time. Carter started the B-1.

"Hope Hawk told the bombers about us!" Elena said.

Carter nodded as he worked at the controls. In the distance, American and Sudanese troop-carrying trucks were racing along the desert track toward the compound.

"What time is it?" Carter shouted as he taxied toward the savanna runway.

"Eleven o'clock!" Elena said, letting out a deep breath.

The ultramodern bomber roared into the air, safe at last, its nuclear weapons beyond the reach of the fanatic Day of the Mahdi group. Carter and Elena looked out their windows at the devastation below. The American and Sudanese troops had moved in and were rounding up the renegade soldiers, hustling them through the smoke and fire off to the barbed wire fence.

The American jets streaked past the B-1, rocking their wings in salute, and Carter's radio squawked.

"Good work!" Hawk's voice boomed. "And thanks!"

THIRTY-TWO

The hotel room in Paris had Wedgwood-blue walls with broad white wainscoting and woodwork. A cut-glass chandelier hung over the bed. A five-pound box of Belgian chocolates was on the bedside table. The card was signed simply "Blenkochev." Mahler's Fifth Symphony played on the stereo phonograph as Nick Carter and Elena Markova sat naked in the king-size bed sipping champagne from a bottle of 1961 Dom Perignon set in a sterling bucket. The card was tied with a red-white-and-blue ribbon to the bottle. It was signed "Hawk."

"I want to tell you more about Leningrad," Elena said, her hand curled on the sheet covering Carter's lap.

"I'm not surprised," Carter said. His arm was across her shoulders, pressing her to him.

"There's a restaurant on the Nevsky Prospekt called Kavkazsky's that I used to go to with a boyfriend," she said. "You don't mind my talking about old boyfriends, do you?"

"As long as they're not present boyfriends," Carter said.

"Good. I wouldn't want to bore you by talking about you." She patted him through the sheet.

"I think I'm too tired," he said.

She felt through the sheet.

"Better tell him, then," she giggled.

"You're too easily distracted," he said, and laughed. "I want to hear about the restaurant. Kavkazsky's?"

"You get the most wonderful food. We must go there

sometime. Spicy Caucasian dishes. Boiled onions, tomatoes, sturgeon, chicken salad, thick, sweet bread, and Georgian wine. Oh! I can taste it just talking about it!''

''And the boyfriend?''

''A party member at the age of twenty-eight. Very dedicated, with eyes so deep they reminded you of the River Neva.''

''You loved him?''

''For a while, but he left me for the party, and I left him for an assignment.'' She shrugged and smiled. ''Life.''

''There will always be assignments,'' Carter said.

''And I hope they all end this well,'' she said.

''Except for Cooley. Damn him. Back in the States with no evidence against him. I couldn't testify. It'd blow my cover. And he can buy or blackmail away any other problems.''

Elena sighed and shook her blond curls.

''At least the Middle East has settled down— the moderate king back in control in Riyadh, Baghdad returned to normal, and Kaddafi lying low.'' Elena drew a circle on the sheet. ''The world is normal again, whatever normal means.''

''It makes one wonder sometimes,'' Carter said, ''when you look at 'normalcy'—our askew values— Beirut, Cambodia . . . all of it . . . is it worth it?''

''There are no answers,'' Elena said, ''only questions.''

''And doing the best we can,'' Carter added. He drank some champagne. ''Here's to us.''

They touched glasses and looked into each other's eyes.

''Have you ever had a love that lasted?'' Elena asked, her voice soft.

''Perhaps as long as yours have.''

They smiled at one another.

''I do think love can last, don't you, Nick? One has to believe that or else what is it all about?''

''It can last, but you have to be together to make it last. Otherwise, it becomes only a memory.''

''I don't have many good memories,'' Elena said,

slipping her head against his neck.

"I know," Carter said, cradling the head. He blew into her golden hair. "It's not part of our jobs."

"I don't want it to be so long between times with you," she said.

He took her champagne goblet and put it and his on the bedside table. He tipped her head back, his thumb under her chin, feeling the velvet skin, and kissed her. She moved into him.

The doorbell rang.

Elena pulled away, her eyes confused and, for a moment, frightened.

"I'll get it," Carter said.

He put on his dressing gown and went to the door.

A bellboy stood outside in a red suit with a matching pillbox hat on his head. He held a vase of hothouse lilacs and peonies, the purples and rich pinks bright against the hall's subdued ivory wallpaper.

"Monsieur Carter?" the bellboy asked.

"Just a minute."

Carter got his billfold and took out a five-dollar bill. He returned to the door and handed the money to the bellboy. The young man stared at the American money, his eyes wide, and gave Carter the fragrant bouquet with respect.

Carter closed the door and carried the flowers to the bed. Mahler's symphony swelled in the room.

"Beautiful!" Elena said, clapping her hands.

"For us," Carter said, opening the card addressed to both of them.

"What does it say?"

" 'I remember, children,' " Carter read and looked up. "It's signed 'Cecil.' "

"He's alive! He made it out!" Elena exclaimed and smiled broadly.

Carter set the bouquet on a table and slid beneath the covers next to Elena's warmth.

"We'll live that long too," Carter said, his lips roaming down Elena's throat to her white breasts. "We have the work." He kissed one. "We have each other now."

He kissed the other. ''And we'll have each other again.''

Elena pulled his head up, her lips hot against his, trembling in his arms, and he spread her legs to make love in the king-size Parisian bed surrounded by music and the scent of flowers.

DON'T MISS THE NEXT NEW NICK CARTER SPY THRILLER

ASSIGNMENT: RIO

"Evenin' . . . buy a lady a drink?"

"Another pint for me, please, and a gin and bitters for the lady."

There was more laughter from the drinkers nearby at the word "lady," and Carter knew it was clear sailing for the night.

In a bar like The Mariner, guts meant everything, even when they were exhibited against an old man by a paunchy Italian.

"Would you be lookin' fer a date, luv?"

"Perhaps."

"They have nice cozy rooms upstairs, they 'ave . . . only five quid and a few bob tip fer the woman who cleans."

Carter put his arm around her thickening middle, and together they slid off the stools. "Lead the way, my dear."

"Don't ya wanna know me price?" she whispered.

"For you, price can be no object."

"My, my, yer a gent, you are!"

Carter didn't miss the high-sign she gave Lindeman as they passed the table. Nor did he miss the Swede's hand tap the shoulder of a swarthy, bull-like man in the booth behind him.

The room was utilitarian at best; a chair, a bedside stand with a wash basin and one dirty towel, and a bed.

"It'll be in advance, luv . . . five quid fer the room, and . . . uh, twenty fer me."

"Twenty? I thought ten would be plenty."

"Ah, now, luv, ain't a bit of a roll with these worth twenty?"

She parted the front of her dress, and two braless mountains of dark-tipped flesh tumbled through the opening.

"Twenty it is," Carter said, pulling a thick wad of notes from his pocket.

He peeled off a twenty and five, and placed them in her hand. Her eyes were so wide with shock and greed that she was paying no attention to the two bills, only to the thick wad in his other hand.

"You get undressed, luv, I'll have to pay fer the room."

"You do that."

She didn't even stuff her breasts back into the dress as she hurried from the room.

Carter moved to the backside of the door, pulled Wilhelmina from the small of his back, flipped her so that the barrel was in his hand, and waited.

It wasn't long, less than two minutes.

The big, dark-skinned man slammed through the door first, with Lindeman close behind him. The Swede went to the right. The big man stood near the foot of the bed, the sap in his right hand hovering to strike.

The butt of the Luger made a sharp crack against the back of his skull, and his body sounded like a felled oak thudding against the bare floor.

Carter kicked the door shut and flipped the gun butt into his palm. In the same movement, he shoved the Luger's ugly snout into the Swede's neck.

"Bijorn Lindeman?"

"Who the hell . . . ?"

"My name doesn't matter, but it's Bellini . . . Salvatore Bellini."

"You move fast for a fat man, Bellini."

"Sit down . . . There!" Carter gestured.

"Up your friggin' . . ."

Carter's backhand caught him flush on the side of the head, sending him sprawling over the bed.

"I am much quicker and stronger than I look, Signore Lindeman. Now please sit quietly and listen to what I have to say."

"You a copper?" Lindeman asked, shaking the bells from his head.

"No."

"Then how do ya know my name?"

"I know a great deal about you, Bijorn Lindeman. You are an ex-convict wanted in three different countries. You are in England now with false papers, but you are trying to bribe your way into a berth aboard the yacht, *Lapita*, sailing for Rio in ten days."

"By God . . ."

Carter took the wad of bills from his pocket and dropped it on the bed. The Swede's eyes watered.

"There is more than enough there to make the bribe. Next week we will meet again. I will give you a package that must go to Rio aboard the *Lapita*."

Lindeman's cracked lips broke into a smile, showing crooked brown teeth.

This was the kind of talk he understood.

—From ASSIGNMENT: RIO
A New Nick Carter Spy Thriller
From Charter in August